ISSUE #16 MARCH 2026

ERIC FLINT'S 1632 & BEYOND

MARC TYRRELL
BETHANNE KIM
JACK CARROLL
NATALIE SILK
JOHN DEAKINS

ERIC FLINT'S 1632 & BEYOND ISSUE #16

This is a work of fiction. Names, characters places, and events portrayed in this book are fictional or used fictitiously. Any resemblance to real people (living or dead), events, or places is coincidental.

Editor-in-Chief Bjorn Hasseler
Production and Design Bethanne Kim
Editor Chuck Thompson
Interior Art Garrett W. Vance

1. Science Fiction-Alternate History
2. Science Fiction-Time Travel

eBook ISBN: 978-1-962398-35-0
Paperback ISBN: 978-1-962398-36-7

Distributed by Flint's Shards Inc.
339 Heyward Street, #200
Columbia, SC 29201

Contents

Eric Flint's 1632 & Beyond

Issue 16

I considered changing the main section of this issue from "Magdeburg Messenger" to "The Low Countries Local." It starts in Flanders, visits along the way, and ends in Flanders. Grantville is here, although parts of only two stories use it as a setting. However, its influence is present in all the stories.

Magdeburg Messenger
(Fiction)

The cover comes from "House Of Verbannen" by Marc Tyrrell. We have been telling the story of Alphons and Désirée in reverse order, beginning with "To Kill A Redbird" in Issue 12, followed by "Adieu, Anvers" in Issue 15, and now "House Of Verbannen." The chronologically later stories fit into themed issues.

The title of "Something New" by Bethanne Kim plays off her story "Something Old" in the previous issue. The story takes place alongside her novels, and you have probably caught some of the hints.

"A Shocking Development" by Jack Carroll is about something so common for us that you may have been trained to use it—but it would make a big difference in the new timeline.

Natalie Silk concludes a series of stories about Anya with "Wild Flowers And Nailed Hearts." Anya, her aunt Dora, uncle Danel, and cousins have appeared in:

"Two Men Walk Into A Beer Garden (Grantville Gazette 81),

"With A Hammer, Everything Is A Nail" (Grantville Gazette 83),

"Anya's Story" (Grantville Gazette 87),

"The Rooster And The Spoon" (Grantville Gazette 92),

"Letting Grace" (Grantville Gazette 95),

"Down This Path" (1632 & Beyond Issue 5),

"A Flask And A Handshake" (1632 & Beyond Issue 12), and

"Green, Blue, And Bruises" (1632 & Beyond Issue 14).

"Antwerp Antics" is the third of John Deakins' stories about famous painters. The first two are "Chiaroscuro" (Grantville Gazette 89) and "Artists From Afar" (1632 & Beyond Issue 14).

Available Now and Coming Soon feature several republished titles and a brand-new novel coming from Baen later this year.

Patreon Supporters

1632 & Beyond thanks the following Patreon members who have generously agreed to help underwrite the magazine's operations.

Thank you so much for supporting us.

Phillip Stewart

Peter Jaeger

Stephanie Walton

Scott W.

Gary

Pascal Durand

Marc Foppen

Sally Hardwick

Karjala Koponen

Jerry Johnson

Marc Tyrrell

David Smith

Edh Stanley

Campbell Menzies

Thomas Williams

Virginia DeMarce

Jay Robison

Chuck Thompson

Magdeburg Messenger

Flint's Shards, Inc.

The House of Verbannen

Marc Tyrrell

Klempf Warehouse, Zülpich
Wednesday, June 11, 1631, 2:45 p.m.

Alphons Verbannen looked at the bodies scattered on the floor like broken, discarded dolls. Shaking his head in disgust, he cleaned his blade on the clothes that Meester Klempf would no longer need before sheathing it. "Did you find the rest of the shipment, Jean-Marc?" he called out.

"Maybe four in five at first glance, Meester Verbannen. I'm still looking."

"Keep looking. We will need a full inventory of what this *varkens neukende klootzak* has here. I'm certain he has other stolen goods." Turning to the man next to him, he asked "Wouldn't you agree, Lieutenant?"

The lieutenant, a sixteen-year-old stripling whose family had bought his commission in the bishop's troops, was still shocked by the carnage. "Ah, yes, of course, Meester Verbannen. The bishop wants to be certain that trade is uninterrupted. And this"—he waved at the bloody scene—"should be a good object lesson to those who would oppose his desires."

Alphons laughed to himself while maintaining a serious face. "I agree, Lieutenant. I need to go through this *klootzak*'s papers. I hope we can find out just where his henchmen are, so that we can clean them out. With writs from both the bishop and the Duke of Julich," and hadn't those cost a bundle in bribes, "we should be able to end this problem once and for all."

Office of the Inspector General, Army of Flanders, Brussels
Thursday, June 12, 1631, 4:30 p.m.

"Don Antonio Manuel Miguel de Godelleta, *Veedor General.*"

Don Luis Phelipe Ladrón de Guevara y Zúñiga, Knight of the Order of Santiago and Inspector General of the Army of Flanders, looked up from the papers he was perusing. "Thank you, Pedro. Come in, Don Antonio. Please,"—he waved at a chair—"sit down. A glass? Rioja? Xérès?"

Antonio glanced at de Guevara, and carefully took his seat. "Xérès, *por favor*. Thank you, Don Luis."

De Guevara waved away his thanks. "Some xérès, if you would, Pedro." The attendant nodded and picked up a decanter and two glasses, setting them on a small table between two chairs. "That will be all." Pedro gave a short bow, turned, and left, closing the door behind him, while de Guevara poured out two glasses of amber xérès, handing one to Antonio, while lifting the other. "To Spain!" Antonio echoed the toast before placing his glass on the table.

De Guevara smiled. "I assume you are wondering why I asked you here today, Don Antonio." It was a statement, not a question. "I have been reviewing the notes of my predecessor, Don Gaspar Ruiz de Perada. He was most impressed by both your honesty and your resourcefulness. I believe that your handling of the situation in Aarschot two years ago also shows your willingness to uphold the honor of Spain."

In August 1629, Antonio had been transferred to the garrison in Aarschot and asked to look into rumors that the garrison commander, Hector de Hevia, was embezzling funds. As a *particulares*, what later generations would call a "Gentleman Ranker", Antonio could be moved between units and had a large degree of freedom. The investigation had been difficult, and Antonio had called upon his uncle Raul and his cousin Alphons for assistance.

Alphons had found solid evidence of embezzlement, but no hard proof that it was being run by the garrison commander. Both Antonio and Alphons were morally certain that he was guilty—he was, after all, living well beyond his means—but without irrefutable evidence, no charges could be laid. Instead, Antonio had taken a leave of absence and ended up fighting a duel with de Hevia. Don Gaspar's assistants had cleared Antonio and found the required proof hidden amongst de Hevia's personal papers. Two other men only referred to as RS and JG were also implicated. "Thank you, Don Luis."

"If you are agreeable, Don Antonio, I would like to move you to one of the tercios under the command of Don Miguel de Manrique." At Antonio's quizzical look, he waved a hand. "No, I do not suspect Don Miguel of peculation. I am, however, concerned about the readiness of his troops. Should we find it desirable to intervene in the Germanies, they will be the ones sent."

Antonio nodded. "I can certainly do that, Don Luis. Is there anything in particular that concerns you?"

De Guevara gave him a careful look, then sighed. "I have no wish to cause you any embarrassment, Don Antonio, so please, I pray you, do not take what I am about to say as anything that impinges on your honor."

Antonio tilted his head, then shrugged. "I shall certainly endeavor not to do so, Don Luis."

De Guevara nodded. "Thank you, Don Antonio." He took a small sip of his xérès, and continued. "You have, I believe, some familiarity with the merchants who supply our troops."

Antonio felt himself tense at that. Implying that a Spanish nobleman, however impoverished, engaged in trade was often cause for an affair of honor. Then he sighed. After all, it was no secret that his uncle Raul was a merchant. He took a small sip of his xérès, then put it back down. "You might say that, Don Luis. I have, shall we say, certain *contacts* amongst the merchants."

De Guevara nodded. "Most excellent, Don Antonio. As I said, I have no concerns about peculation. I do, however, have some concerns about the—shall we say 'quality'?—of some of the supplies that are being sold to General de Manrique's troops. Nothing solid, really, just rumors on the breeze," he shrugged.

De Guevara paused. "What I would ask of you is that you keep your eyes and ears open, and let me know if there is any truth to these rumors. If there is, I would like to know if you think it is intentional or accidental." Don Antonio nodded. "And let me also say that if it *is* intentional, then that merchant will no longer be selling to us."

Antonio thought about that. *I'd best stop in Huldenberg on the way, and talk with Uncle Raul.* "I will see what I can discover, Don Luis."

De Guevara leaned back and smiled. "Excellent! I look forward to reading your report." He reached over and handed Antonio a folded piece of paper. "Here are your orders, signed by Don Pedro de San Juan himself, so there should be no difficulties."

Pedro de San Juan was the Secretary of State and War under Infanta Isabella, so no one would question his orders. Indeed, having Don Pedro sign those orders implied that Antonio was a *compadre*, someone who needed to be taken seriously, with friends in high places. That signature gave Antonio more leeway than he would normally have. "Thank you, Don Luis. And please, convey my gratitude and respect to Don Pedro."

Verbannen Huis, Huldenberg, Flanders
Friday, June 13, 1631, 2:05 p.m.

When Raul Rafael departed Spain at the direction of his father for his "un-noble" attitude, he had taken a remittance, moved to the Spanish Netherlands, and changed his name to Verbannen. There, he had met Maaike Ouwerx, the daughter of a Flemish merchant, and they had wed in 1591. Alphons, his eldest son, had appeared the year after, in April of 1592.

Since then, the family had prospered, supplying the tercios coming to the Spanish Netherlands, and also investing in other businesses and trading ventures. Today, their network of business contacts stretched from Milan, through Tyrol, Bavaria, the Rhineland, Franconia and, of course, throughout the Spanish Netherlands and the Dutch Republic. Despite being "in business", Raul had stayed in communication with his eldest brother, whose son, Antonio, sat before him.

"So, let me make certain that I understand you correctly. You want me to spy on my competitors based on nothing but vague rumors?" Raul Verbannen stared at Antonio, who was nervously shifting in his seat.

"It's all I have, Uncle Raul."

Raul just shook his head. "Do you happen to have a list of de Manrique's suppliers and what they supplied?" Antonio nodded and handed Raul a small sheet of paper, which he started to peruse. "Well, that's something at any rate. Hmmm," he said as he worked his way down the list, then looked up again. "Well, I know several of the people on this list personally, and most by reputation." Raul cocked his head. "What type of company are you going to?"

"Muskets, Uncle Raul."

"And are there other *particulares* in that company?"

"Probably." Antonio shrugged. "I won't really know until I get there, but I wouldn't be surprised. You know how we tend to get put into the same companies."

Raul was nodding. "True, but it also creates a bit of a difficulty for you. If someone *is* playing games with your supplies, it won't be with any of those companies, unless they are incredibly foolish." Raul tapped his fingers on the table, then gave a slight shrug. "Well, you're posted where you're posted but, if I were you, I would try and make friends with some of the musketeers in the pike companies."

"I think I understand your reasoning, Uncle. I'm just not sure why you made that point."

Raul tapped one name on the list. "This one, *Meester* Dievout, has a good reputation, but as a reseller of goods, not a producer. He is known to be careful in his initial purchases, but somewhat over-trusting in his later ones. And he has the contract for providing most of the powder to de Manrique's troops. High value, low bulk, and not used overly much in garrison. That is a situation ripe with possibilities."

Antonio thought about that and nodded. "An excellent point, Uncle, and I already have an idea about how I can go about getting samples. Can you ask Alphons if he would be able to help me in, say, about two weeks?"

Raul's eyes flicked upwards, then back down. "It may be three weeks. Alphons is looking into something for me in Cologne." Raul smiled somewhat wryly. "I suspect you will need some extra resources for your investigation." Raul knew that Antonio was, if not impoverished, then living mainly through his pay. He took out a purse and slid it across the table. "There's twenty-five guilders in there. *Do* try not to lose it in a single card game!"

Verbannen Huis, Huldenberg, Flanders
Thursday, June 26, 1631, 1:05 p.m.

"How was it, Alphons?"

Alphons, who was relaxing, shrugged. "Not too bad, Father. Klempf had hired a bunch of mercenaries and was fencing the goods they took. Once we found him, and his records, it was simple." Alphons shrugged. "The bishop has sent us a 'well done' which, when all is considered, *might* buy a small beer. I had to spend over four hundred guilders, but we got them. They won't prey on us, or anyone else, anymore."

Raul nodded. "Good. Four hundred guilders is nothing compared to the message you sent, and both the Duke and the bishop will owe us." He leaned back. "I've got another project for you involving your cousin Antonio...."

De Manrique's camp, Antonio's company area, Flanders
Saturday, June 28, 1631, 11:25 a.m.

Alphons Verbannen looked around, trying to spot his cousin. At five foot ten inches and two hundred pounds, almost all of it muscle, Alphons looked nothing like Antonio, who was three inches shorter and forty pounds lighter. Alphons heard occasional shots being fired, and then a loud cheer off to his left and decided to check it out. As he approached, he saw Antonio laughing and slapping a rather shabbily clad musketeer on the shoulder, with another twenty or so people standing around talking.

"Alphons! Come on over and meet Bastião. This *hijo de puta* just beat me in a shooting match." Antonio was smiling as he spoke.

Alphons raised his eyebrows in surprise as he walked over. Antonio was an excellent shot, even with a smoothbore musket. When he was about five feet away, he stopped and gave a small bow, more of a nod really, in Antonio's direction. "Don Antonio, wonderful to see you as always."

Turning to Bastião, he nodded, smiled, and held out his hand. "Congratulations, Bastião. Don Antonio is a fine marksman, so to have bested him is a real feat. I'm Alphons Verbannen."

"Bastião Diaz, Sir."

Alphons waved that away. "Please, call me Alphons. Everyone does." He was beaming with good will, but his eyes were evaluating Bastião. *His clothes are in terrible shape, and he looks like he hasn't eaten well in months. Something stinks, here.*

"Alphons, please tell me that you have found some xérès?" Antonio said with a patently false pleading look on his face. Turning to Bastião, he confided, "I count on Alphons to find anything I really need. He is a most resourceful fellow, who seems to know everyone who has anything worth having."

Bastião was starting to look trapped, so Alphons said smoothly, "He's correct, Bastião." Alphons' smile grew into a grin. "Besides that, anyone who can outshoot Don Antonio deserves a reward." He turned to face Antonio. "And, yes, I have your xérès. I actually came here today to invite you for dinner tonight at *De Rode Haan*. Please, can you come?"

Antonio nodded. "Of course, Alphons." He reached into his purse and pulled out a guilder. Turning to Bastião, he said "Here's the prize I promised you." His face took on a good-natured scowl "And the next time we shoot, I plan on beating you."

Alphons laughed. "Maybe you should ask him to give you lessons, Don Antonio?" Antonio started to sputter, while Alphons grinned. "But enough of these pleasantries! Don Antonio, I hope to see you for dinner at, say, Vespers?" Antonio grinned wryly and nodded. Alphons turned to Bastião. "And you, my friend have earned a reward! Not only for your shooting, but for knocking my cousin off his high horse. Come, let us go to your camp and we can talk about what you would like!"

De Rode Haan common room,

5:55 p.m.

Antonio strode into the common room at *De Rode Haan* with a satchel over his shoulder and an insouciant grin on his face. Spotting Alphons reading at a small table in the back corner, he walked over and sat down, carelessly reaching for a cup. "Evening, Alphons."

Alphons looked up and gave him a curt smile. "Evening, Antonio. What did you bring me?"

Antonio handed the satchel to him. "I've got powder samples from twelve different companies." Seeing the look in Alphons' eyes, he nodded. "Yes, they are all marked as to which company they come from."

Alphons gave a tight smile. "Good." He reached over and poured wine into his own mug, draining it in one gulp, before refilling it and placing it on the table. He stared at Antonio. "Someone, and I mean to find out who, is supplying shoddy goods." He leaned back and took a deep breath, letting it out slowly. "I went with Bastião to his camp, and what I saw and heard there made me want to kill someone."

Antonio studied his cousin while he sipped his own wine. "That bad?"

Alphons snorted. "Let's see. Weevils in newly delivered flour. Meat that is just on the edge, or over. Sour beer, and poorly made cloth. And they are being charged for quality goods. Someone is pocketing a *lot* of money." He shook his head in disgust. "I talked with the camp followers there, and everyone told me that this is coming from the main commissariat."

"*Bueno joder*!" Antonio leaned back and thought. "De Manrique?"

Alphons shook his head. "I doubt it. If it were him, we'd see the same pattern across all of the companies, and I haven't heard anything that would lead me to conclude that."

Antonio started to nod. "Good point. I've visited some of the other companies, and things seemed fine there."

Alphons grinned, but it was twisted, marring his face. "Lots of *particulares* in those companies?"

Antonio shrugged. "Sure. A couple of us will go to drink wine and play cards. Not much else to do when you're in garrison."

"It's a rough life, Antonio. Deal with it." His face cleared. "I'm sending Bastião's company some food tomorrow so they can have a victory celebration." He shrugged. "Nothing much, really: a couple of sheep, a hundredweight of good wheat flour, and some beer. Make sure you go—and stay in touch with him."

Antonio just shook his head. "I *do* know how to build informant networks, Alphons. I'll be there. What are you going to be doing?"

Alphons chuckled. "Getting these powder samples tested and finding out just who is providing what to these troops. I'll be back in a week or so."

Verbannen Huis, Huldenberg, Flanders
Tuesday, July 1, 1631, 3:45 p.m.

Raul Verbannen looked up as his eldest son walked into the room, face wreathed in storm clouds. "That bad, Alphons?"

Alphons just nodded and sat down. "I've got the test results on the powder. Every company with lots of *particulares* had acceptable powder. The others?" he shrugged. "Calling it trash is an insult to garbage." He leaned forward. "The alchemist who did the analysis told me that they had cut the powder with sawdust *before* it was corned."

Raul winced. "*Eso está jodido*! Do you think *Meester* Dievout is responsible?"

Alphons shrugged. "Maybe? At least inasmuch as his oversight is lax. But if the powder was adulterated *before* he bought it, which it must have been, then his only 'crime' was to assume quality."

Raul nodded slowly, a twisted smile on his face. "Dievout is, unfortunately, known for making that assumption." He leaned back and searched for a paper. "I asked *Meester* De Vos if he knew who was providing *Meester* Dievout with powder. In between some rather extraordinary invective, he pointed me towards a *Meester* Vizard. He's located in Herentals."

Alphons smiled grimly. "I'll head over there and see what I can find out. What about the other suppliers?"

Raul smiled slightly in return. "*Meester* De Smedt and *Meester* Baert are the two main suppliers of general goods."

"*Uncle Adrienne*?"

"Yes, Adrienne Baert." Raul frowned. "I've known Adrienne for a long time, and I can't see him knowingly doing something like what you have reported. You need to visit him and see just what is going on."

Alphons nodded and made a mental note. "Fine, I'll do that. What about de Smedt?"

Raul shrugged. "I don't know much about him, but what I do know leads me to believe that he is...less than the soul of probity."

"Corrupt?"

"Probably more than most," Raul replied with a razor grin. "I have a list of people who have dealt with him you should talk with." Raul slid a sheet of paper over the table to Alphons. "How's Antonio doing?"

Alphons chuckled. "He's running his 'Can you outshoot me?' scam. That's how he got the powder samples. From what he said, he's only lost three times out of twelve; twice to other *particulares*." Alphons leaned forward. "The third person he lost to, one Bastião Diaz, is from one of the pike companies. I came into the camp just after Antonio lost and got to meet him. His situation is interesting.

"His clothes were threadbare, and he looked undernourished. Once I followed him back to his camp, I understood why. He, and his company, were being supplied with garbage and paying full price for it." Alphons closed his eyes, trying to control the surge of anger he felt. "I sent them enough for a 'victory feast' but, Father, that will probably be the best meal they have had in months.

"The camp followers told me that it was what the commissariat provided and they weren't allowed to buy outside of it." His eyes were hooded, staring into the distance. Raul was reminded of a raptor before it struck. "Someone there is on the take and, when we find him, I want a couple of minutes with him. Alone."

"You know, Alphons, there are times you remind me of my grandfather." Raul's tone was light, but focused. "Do *try* not to kill anyone. Unless they deserve it."

Meester Vizard's powder mill, outside Herentals
Thursday, July 3, 1631, 4:45 p.m.

"As you can see, Meester Verbannen, we produce roughly two hundredweight of coarse powder, along with ten to twelve pounds of fine-grained powder every week, all of the finest quality."

There is no way you can produce that much! You can't possibly get enough saltpeter, Alphons thought as he smiled and nodded towards *Meester* Vizard's senior journeyman. "That is most impressive, sir, most impressive! We are exploring an opportunity that would involve, shall we say, a hundredweight of coarse and five pounds of fine powder every month. Would you be able to meet such a requirement?"

The journeyman was nodding. "I fully expect so, Meester Verbannen. And given those amounts, we would be happy to arrange a direct delivery to your customer at no extra charge."

Alphons was smiling and nodding. *So* that's *how you bypassed Dievout!* "That would be most agreeable. Well, if I might have some samples—shall we say ten charges?—I will be in touch with you as soon as this opportunity firms up."

Baert Huis, Zandhoven, Flanders
Friday, July 4, 1631, 1:15 p.m.

Alphons stared up at the front of the house he had spent so much time in as a child, with a wistful smile on his face. *Really, Alphons, you could have come here any time in the past decade, but...* His thought trickled away. *Enough of this!* He squared his shoulders, walked up the stairs, and used the door knocker.

After a moment, the door was opened by an old man in upper servant's garb. "Yes, may I help...Young Master Alphons? Is that you?"

Alphons grinned. "It is indeed, Jean! I am glad to see you again."

Jean pulled the door wider and gestured for Alphons to enter. "Come in, come in! Oh, it is grand to see you again! It must be, what, six years?"

Alphons chuckled as he entered. "Closer to ten I believe, Jean." He got a wicked grin on his face. "I swear to the Blessed Virgin, you haven't aged a day since the last time I saw you!"

Jean let out a sound halfway between a snort and a laugh. "I could wish, Master Alphons! But, let me take your hat and cloak." Alphons doffed them, and Jean whisked them away. "You'll be wanting to see Master Baert, I assume?" At Alphons' nod, he continued. "Well, you've come at an auspicious time; this is one of his good days."

At Alphons' raised eyebrow, Jean continued in a quiet voice. "Master Baert is not now the man you remember. He has had *problems,* shall we say, with his memory for the past year and a bit." Jean shook his head. "And I fear that Master Dirk is, ah, not of as much assistance as might have been expected."

Alphons frowned as they walked. "Hasn't Dirk picked up some of the load? I know that Uncle Adrienne had trained him to take over the business."

Jean looked around carefully, then spoke in a very low voice that didn't carry. "Master Dirk has been...pursuing other interests, and Master Luc has been apprenticing in Antwerp. Most of the day-to-day operations of the business are in the hands of Geert de Zele, Master Baert's general factor."

Alphons' frown deepened. "And is de Zele not doing a good job?"

Jean shrugged as they climbed the stairs, moving towards Adrienne Baert's study. "Who knows? *I* don't—but I do *not* like the man. There is something about him that *disturbs* me. Nothing seen, just a feeling, if you know what I mean."

Alphons nodded.

* * *

"So, Alphons, why are you here?" Dirk Baert was pushing his food around the plate, eating little, but drinking much.

"Oh, you know how it is, Dirk. Work, work, work! Father has me chasing around all over the place." Alphons took a forkful of the meat and stilled his reaction. *Bah! My cook would never serve this!* He glanced over at Adrienne Baert, who seemed to be eating with every indication of acceptance.

Dirk popped a piece of beef in his mouth and grimaced, even as he chewed it and swallowed, followed by a full glass of wine, which was immediately refilled. "You need a break, Alphons. Look, I'm heading out after dinner to a private club. Why don't you come along?"

Adrienne looked up, a slight frown on his face. "You're not going to be gone all night, are you? We have some contracts to look over in the morning, and I want you there."

Dirk waved his hand, sloshing wine onto the table. "No, I'll be back early, Father. Probably by midnight. Besides that, Alphons needs a break, and you wouldn't begrudge him some relaxation, would you?"

"No, no. You boys have fun." Adrienne forked up another piece of beef and started to chew it. "Just..." his voice tapered off.

"We'll be back soon, Uncle Adrienne. And, I am sure, Dirk will be ready for whatever you need him for in the morning." Alphons choked down another piece of over-cooked beef.

De Oprechte Mens, Antwerp

9:14 p.m.

Alphons was not unfamiliar with either brothels or gaming houses, but neither was he an *habitué. De Oprechte Mens* combined both in a lavish environment, with a large salon opening on the right hand of the entryway full of tables and people playing cards, and a smaller salon on the left, displaying the house's wares. At five guilders, the entry fee was steep, but Alphons had been assured that that price included *all* of the evening's entertainment. Alphons had merely smiled and handed over the coins, while Dirk made for the smaller room, looking around.

Alphons shook his head ruefully and strolled after Dirk. As he entered, he could see that many of the people in the small salon knew Dirk. Nothing overt, but carefully controlled expressions spoke volumes. One young woman in particular, with lovely auburn hair and a heart-shaped face, was less controlled, showing a flash of disdain before she smoothed out her expression as her eyes went towards Alphons, giving him a professional smile which Alphons returned.

Alphons casually glanced around and saw Dirk talking with a very young woman. His eyes narrowed for a moment as he focused on the girl, before glancing quickly at her wrists. *Twelve, maybe thirteen and, if I'm not mistaken, that's a boy. Dirk what in the name of the Blessed Virgin are you doing?* He saw Dirk hold out his hand and lead the child upstairs.

His eyes returned to the auburn-haired woman and he sauntered over to give her a short bow. "*Mejuffrouw*, allow me to introduce myself. My name is Alphons, and I am a visitor in your fair city. I wonder if you might be interested in some wine and quiet conversation? Possibly in a more secluded locale?"

The smile on her face was all professional, not reaching her eyes. "Please call me Désirée, Alphons. And yes, some wine and *conversation* would be a welcome diversion." She stood up and signaled a servant, speaking to him quietly and receiving a nod in reply. Turning back to Alphons, she gave him the same smile. "Shall we? The wine will be brought soon."

Alphons' smile reached his eyes, but showed a sense of both understanding and empathy. "Please, lead the way."

She nodded and led him up the stairs and into a chamber several doors down. As he entered, Alphons could see a large bed and, somewhat surprisingly, two chairs with a shared table adjacent to them. "Please, Alphons, sit down. I expect that..." A knock on the door interrupted her, and she opened it, waving inside a servant carrying a flagon of wine and two goblets. He placed them on the table, gave Alphons a short bow, then left, closing the door behind him. Désirée walked over and poured wine into the goblets, handing one to Alphons before sitting in the other chair.

Alphons waited until she was seated and raised his goblet in a toast towards her. "To fortune; may ours always be good." She raised her goblet in return but her eyes showed clearly that her fortunes had not always prospered. Alphons took a sip, then placed his goblet on the table and cleared his throat. "I couldn't help but note, when I came in, that you appeared to be less than enthralled with my companion." He raised an eyebrow. "Might I ask why?"

Désirée raised her eyebrows in return, then slowly sipped her wine while she examined Alphons. Finally, she gave a slight shrug. "I have only the *pleasure* of a slight acquaintance with *Meester* Baert. He has increasingly preferred *conversational* opportunities with others over the past year, as you may have noticed."

Alphons gave her a wry grin. "I did notice that. He seemed to be...signally focused on, shall we say, a limited repertoire of discourse this evening."

Désirée suppressed a smile that, this time, actually reached her eyes. "Yes, I have noticed that his taste in conversational partners has, oh, how shall I put this? Ah, yes, tended towards the *younger* members of this house." She gave a slight shrug that accentuated certain of her features, before losing her smile. "I believe that the owner of this establishment, *Meester* de Zele, has been encouraging him in these pursuits."

"Geert de Zele?"

Désirée raised an eyebrow. "Why, yes. Do you know him?" There was a look of fear in her eyes.

Alphons shook his head. "I am merely aware of him. I cannot say that I have ever met the man and, from many things I hear about him, I am unsure as to whether I wish to."

The fear left Désirée's eyes as she started to nod. "He can be...difficult, especially if his wishes are thwarted." She reached over and patted Alphons' hand in a friendly manner. "You would be well-advised to steer clear of him, Alphons."

* * *

Désirée kissed him, slowly, something he knew to be exceedingly rare in her profession. "Alphons, be careful." She stared into his eyes, and all he saw there was concern for him. "Please avoid de Zele if you can. He can be...direct if challenged." A slight smile flitted over her face. "And I would be sorry to lose such a wonderful conversational partner."

Alphons' return smile warmed her. "I will be careful, of that you can be assured. Hmmm," his brow furrowed as he hesitated, thinking. "Désirée, I will probably be leaving tomorrow." Her eyes clouded at that. "Still, I would hope that we might remain in contact and," his smile grew mischievous, "that we might engage in further conversations in the future." Now his smile grew wistful. "I fear that I have had few such since my wife died eight years ago, and I do cherish them." He looked into her eyes. "Might I leave you the wherewithal to contact me?"

Surprise, and some other emotion that Alphons couldn't identify—Hope? Fear? Astonishment?—flashed across her face. "I...I would like that." She studied his face closely. "Would you truly wish to contact me outside of these walls?"

Alphons heard his father's voice in the back of his mind yelling, *Are you insane?!?!,* and didn't care. *She may be a whore, Father, but she is worried about my fate.* "I would, Désirée. Do you have access to a quill, ink, and paper?"

She looked stunned, but nodded. "In the drawer on the table."

Alphons got up, pulled out the writing implements and proceeded to write a short list. "The top address is my home; anything sent to me there will, eventually, reach me. The next address is my banker in Antwerp. If you show him this paper, he will assist you." Alphons handed her the page. "And now," he sighed and closed his eyes, "I suppose I must really be going." He stood up and started towards the door.

Désirée started to chuckle. "You might want to get dressed first, Alphons."

* * *

Alphons watched the card game in front of him, not allowing his perceptions to show. *Two of them are colluding to fleece Dirk,* he thought, as the game of Primero moved into its final phase. Dirk was smiling as he laid down his cards, and started to reach for the pot. "Fluxus."

The opponent across from him smiled, and laid down four kings. "Chorus." He swept the pot, which must have contained a hundred guilders, towards him. "Tough luck, my friend! But the night is still young. Shall we try another hand?"

Alphons moved closer to the table and spoke. "Dirk, I believe you have an appointment in the morning. Early. We should go."

Dirk snarled and glared at Alphons. "I was planning on staying for at least another two hours. Why leave now?"

Alphons showed him a mild face, merely stating, "Well, and we have an hour's ride in front of us. By the time we are home, it will be closer to Lauds than Matins."

Dirk seemed to deflate, then let out a sigh. "I suppose, Alphons." Shaking his head, he continued. "It's not like Dame Fortuna was smiling on me tonight anyway." He pushed back his chair, and gave a short bow to the table. "Until next time." He turned and walked out, followed by Alphons.

Laurids Huis, Antwerp
Sunday, July 6, 1631, 2:15 p.m.

Alphons walked into Samuel Laurid's office, feeling somewhat off balance. Samuel took one look at him then, waving the servant away, poured two glasses of wine, handing one to Alphons and indicating a chair. "Sit down, my friend." Samuel's eyes scoured Alphons. "Unless my eyes deceive me, you are carrying a heavy burden. Please, tell me how I can help." Samuel sat down and sipped his wine.

Alphons gave him a tired smile. "I am afraid I am in over my head, Samuel." He sipped the wine, eyes widening. "Kosher?"

Samuel nodded with a slight smile. "Of course. Would you expect anything else?" Alphons had first met Samuel fifteen years ago when they had concluded several mutually beneficial business arrangements. Twelve years prior, Alphons had discovered that Samuel was a *marrano*, a "secret Jew" who professed the Catholic faith, but still practiced his own. Ten years ago, Samuel had introduced Alphons, standing surety for him, to a correspondence network that passed information on religious toleration throughout Europe.

"Not at all. Would you arrange an introduction for me with the vintner? I can think of several people who would appreciate this vintage."

Samuel smiled. "Of course." The smile disappeared. "But what is this talk about being 'in over your head'? I have never known you to be less than resourceful, my friend." He took a sip of his wine, waiting for Alphons' answer.

Alphons sighed, then shook his head. "It all started when my cousin, Antonio, approached my father."

Samuel rolled his eyes. "Didn't you learn anything after Aarschot?"

Alphons grinned crookedly. "And what would you do if Don Luis Phelipe Ladrón de Guevara y Zúñiga asked *you* to look into something? Yes, I knew it might be troublesome, but...it...." He sighed and waved his hands.

Samuel nodded in comprehension of Alphons' plight. Don Luis was, after all, a power in the Spanish Netherlands, and one did not refuse his requests lightly. Samuel sighed. "What do you need, Alphons?"

Alphons finished his glass of wine. "Three, no, four things, Samuel. I need whatever you can find out about three men: Jan Vizard, Claes de Smedt, and Geert de Zele." Seeing the quickly hidden wince on Samuel's face, he continued. "I take it you know of some of them?"

"I know de Zele. He is, well, let me just say that I hope you are not entering into any arrangements with him."

Alphons looked at him. "No, I am not planning to do so. However, he is Adrienne Baert's general manager, and Adrienne is an old friend of my father's." Alphons' eyes slitted. "I am afraid that Uncle Adrienne has become, ah, somewhat 'forgetful'."

Samuel parsed that statement. "I believe that de Zele is, in many ways, in control of Baert's company. He has several other interests that are somewhat less savory." Samuel's eyes flicked up, then down. "I have a file on him, and I can arrange for it to be updated and sent to you."

"Thank you, Samuel. Do you know anything about Vizard or de Smedt?"

Samuel shrugged. "Not at the moment, but give me a week or two and I can have something for you." He cocked his head to the side. "Is anything else concerning you?"

Samuel was amused, then concerned, to notice a flush rising up Alphons' face. "Ah, yes. I, ah, gave your name to a fr...informant named Désirée. She may contact you and, if she does, please do whatever she asks." Alphons' face assumed a wry grin, "Well, up to a cost of a hundred guilders." He leaned forward. "If she needs to contact me, please advise her of my latest address: she already has Verbannen Huis."

Samuel's eyebrows shot up at both the amount and at Alphons' look. His lips quivered, and he started shaking his head. "Why do I think that Don Alphons Quixote rides again?" He gave out a sound halfway between a sigh and a chortle as he saw Alphons' blush deepening. "Fine, I will do so. Do you expect her to contact me?"

Alphons shrugged. "I don't know. Perhaps? But, if she does, I expect that she will need immediate aid."

De Oprechte Mens, Antwerp

3:00 p.m.

Geert de Zele was in his office going over the receipts from the previous week, while his manager, Lucretia, lounged, sipping wine and languidly reading a book. At five foot eight inches, Lucretia was extremely tall for a woman but, since she had been named 'Luc' at her baptism, that was unsurprising. Something snagged de Zele's eye, and he started to frown.

"Lucretia, why is Dirk Baert's letter of hand so low? I only see charges for some sixty guilders? Was he *that* lucky at the table?"

Lucretia raised her eyes languidly from the book she was reading. "He left earlier than usual. And, no, his luck is the same as always; what we decide it to be."

De Zele leaned back, frowning. "Why would he leave early? He usually spends the night here."

"Oh, some friend he brought reminded him of a meeting and dragged him away early." Lucretia shrugged while de Zele digested that.

"And does that *friend* have a name?"

Lucretia furrowed her eyebrows. "I am certain he does, but I heard nothing more than Alphons, and that he was an old family friend." She looked into de Zele's eyes. "You would probably know better than I would."

"I will make enquiries tomorrow," he said, making a mental note to do so. "And what did this *Alphons* do? Did he sit at cards?"

Lucretia allowed a salacious smile to grow. "No, he spent several hours with one of the girls."

De Zele nodded. "Send for her."

* * *

Désirée walked into the study, trying to mask her trepidation at being called.

De Zele looked up, while Lucretia merely gazed at her, pointing to a chair set in front of de Zele. "So, Désirée. I hear you spent quite some time with young Baert's companion." De Zele's voice was controlled, giving nothing away.

"Several hours, Meester de Zele."

"And what did you learn of him?"

Désirée tilted her head, frowning slightly. "Learn of him? Not much. His name is Alphons. He claimed to be an old friend of the Baert family, and is a merchant of some type. I believe he said something about leaving the next day, but as to where, or why, I have no idea."

"Describe him to me."

Désirée called up a mental image and suppressed a smile. "He is tall, maybe five foot ten inches, and in his late thirties or early forties. Rather heavy; maybe two hundred pounds. Dark brown hair, with rather startling blue eyes set in a squarish face."

De Zele's eyes flicked towards Lucretia, who nodded. "And does he bear any scars or distinguishing marks?"

"A long-healed scar from a sword or knife on his right chest, and a few small scars such as a man might have from a slipped knife. Nothing else." She shrugged.

De Zele nodded in thought. "Alright, Désirée. Go up to the Gold Room, I will join you shortly." He reveled in the slight spurt of fear he saw in her eyes, quickly suppressed.

De Oprechte Mens, Antwerp
Monday, July 7, 1631, 3:15 a.m.

Désirée lay on her bed, unable to sleep. She was still in agony from her encounter with de Zele, and the three additional clients she had serviced that night added to the pain. *You're not getting out of here alive, girl.* She sighed, and turned to her other side. She had, she knew, been lucky. Lucky to have been in a convent school for two years before her parents were tried and executed as heretics, along with her brother. Lucky that the Mother Superior had defended her. And lucky that she had listened to her mother in the matter of what herbs would allow a woman to avoid pregnancy.

And there her luck had ended. With her parents' estate being taken to cover court costs, there was no money left for her to either attend school or join the convent. And so, at the age of fifteen, she found herself adrift in the world with few resources, and no family. She had tried to find a position, any position, but failed. Meeting Geert de Zele had seemed like a dream come true, with his promises of a better life in Antwerp, and she had willingly signed a ten-year indenture contract, having no concept of what she was getting into.

A slight smile curved her lips as she thought of Alphons, and she stifled a giggle as she thought about him striding to the doorway, naked. After dressing, he had left her two guilders and stressed again that she should contact him if and when she chose. *After eight years here, I should know better, but....* the thought drifted off into a haze of wishful thinking, of what might have been. She let out a sigh and tried to sleep.

De Rode Haan common room
Tuesday, July 8, 1631, 6:25 p.m.

"Alphons, good to see you. Finally!" Antonio sat down at the table and poured himself a mug of wine. "Where in the name of the Blessed Virgin have you been? It's been almost two weeks!"

Alphons raised an eyebrow and started to chuckle. "I've been riding a lot, Antonio. Honestly, my arse feels like one of those pounded steaks from Hamburg!" He looked at his cousin, who was lounging and smiling. "So, what have you found out?"

Antonio's smile grew larger and took on a vicious cast, as he pulled a piece of paper from his courier pouch and slid it over to Alphons. "The names of four clerks in the commissariat who are most adamant that they are the only ones who may supply the troops, and the name of their quartermaster general."

Alphons raised both eyebrows. "Been busy, haven't you?"

Antonio grinned widely. "Bastião was kind enough to introduce me to some of his friends in other pike companies." The grin slid from his face. "Most seem to be in the same predicament he is. I, ah, took the liberty of suggesting that you might send suitable victory feasts to several other companies." Antonio looked abashed.

Alphons snorted a laugh. "Got beaten again? By how many?" Antonio mumbled something. "Sorry, I couldn't hear that. How many did you say?"

Antonio glared at him. "Five. *Five* times, Alphons! *Five fucking times*!"

Alphons looked at Antonio' and started laughing, finally having to stifle it by putting his hand over his mouth. "The great Don Antonio brought low...by FIVE rankers!" he started laughing again, while Antonio glared at him, then started to chuckle.

Finally, Antonio waved his hand. "Fine, yes, five times." His face sobered. "Will you send them something? Help me redeem my word?"

Alphons was still smiling, but nodded. "Of course. Give me the list of companies, and I'll arrange for it tomorrow." His smile faded. "How are you handling it now?"

Antonio smiled. "I've managed to get several of the boys to agree to a Marksmen's League. They're coughing up about fifteen guilders, and think it's great sport." Sobering, he added, "You know, it's actually a really good idea, and good for morale."

Alphons was nodding. "Good, glad to hear it. And," he waved the pieces of paper, "I am *very* glad to get these."

Antonio's face was now completely focused. "And how is the rest of the investigation going?"

Alphons' smile was razor sharp. "I need a week, week and a half, to wrap up my end of it." He sighed and leaned back. "I still have some people to talk to and a number of reports to get, but I have a very good idea of what is going on here."

De Oprechte Mens, Antwerp
Monday, July 14, 1631, 2:10 a.m.

Désirée finally let her weakness show as she undressed and got ready for bed. Thankfully, the crowd had been light tonight, but that *moederverdomde klootzak* de Zele had used her again this afternoon, and she had been hard-put to show even a professional smile to the clients tonight. The one client she had this evening, Marc Jacobs, a regular, had taken one look at her and told her that he would be with her for the rest of the evening. *He really is a dear, even if he is old enough to be my grandfather!* They had spent the evening drinking wine, talking, and playing chess.

She thought back to his reaction as he saw how she winced when she moved and sat. His eyes had widened, and he had said *Girl, you have to get out of here. I'd offer you a place, but....*his blush said it all. She knew his wife accepted him coming here, but drew the line at him supporting a mistress. *He really is a dear,* she thought as she looked at the guilder he had given her, along with a further entreaty for her to leave.

She sighed as she pulled the covers aside and slid into the bed after carefully secreting the guilder with the rest of her money. *Is Marc correct? Should I leave?* She twitched her body, trying to find a comfortable position, but pain kept stabbing through her. Finally, the pain subsided enough that she was able to think clearly. A memory of Marc's comment, *Girl, you have to get out of here*, segued into Alphons' comment as he left: *Contact me at any time.*

Désirée's brow furrowed as she thought. *Alphons is going after de Zele, even after I warned him off. Something in his eyes said he wouldn't leave well enough alone.* She rolled onto her other side. *Could he actually* best *de Zele?* She savored that thought.

Maybe. She sighed and shifted positions again, trying to think. *Blessed Virgin*, she prayed, *help me find my way through this morass!* Slowly, a picture of de Zele's study formed in her mind, and centered on his account books. Désirée felt herself growing cold and heard, faintly, a calm voice saying "The crossroad is here. Life, death, or ambivalence. The choice is yours"*!*

The cold spread through her body under the warm blankets, wrapping her in a certainty that she didn't want. Terror filled her, but she now knew what she had to do. *Be careful what you pray for....*

3:05 a.m.

Désirée, wearing her oldest dress, with her few belongings and shoes packed in a small bag, tiptoed down the back stairs towards the kitchen. She knew that while the door to the study from the parlor was locked every night, they rarely bothered to lock the door from the kitchen to the study. As she passed through the kitchen, she took a candle and lit it from the banked coals in the hearth, then set out for the door to the study.

The acrid scent of fear clogged her nostrils as she tried the door. *Blessed Virgin, PLEASE let it be unlocked!* The latch lifted and the door swung open silently. *Thank You!* Désirée entered, closing the door behind her, and walked over to the shelves holding the ledgers. She took four, which filled her bag. She rapidly retreated to the kitchen, replaced the candle and blew it out, then unbarred the back door, opened it, and left, closing it silently behind her.

Laurids Huis, Antwerp
5:15 a.m.

Désirée timidly knocked on the imposing door at the address she had been given. No answer. She knocked louder, desperately praying that she was doing the right thing. Finally, the door opened, and a sleepy looking, but large, doorman looked at her and said, "We are not open, come back in two hours," and started to close the door on her.

She inserted a foot into the gap, wincing as the door hit it. "I am here to see *Meester* Laurids, at the behest of *Meester* Alphons Verbannen." The pressure on her foot relaxed and the door opened, showing a glowering face.

"Fine. Go into the parlor, and I will let *Meester* Laurids know you are here." He glared at her, raking her body with his eyes. "Who shall I say is calling?"

Désirée, feeling his disdain, put on her professional face and replied. "Tell him that Désirée, a friend of *Meester* Verbannen, wishes to talk with him."

The doorman harrumphed, but showed her into the parlor. She looked around the room, eyes widening as she recognized the wealth it represented. She wandered over to a bookcase and started to look at the titles. *My goodness! There must be several hundred books here!* She recognized titles by Aquinas and other great Catholic theologians, along with the works of Homer, Cicero, Virgil, and Caesar.

Taking down a volume of Cicero, she sat in a chair and opened it, slowly working her way through the Latin text. She was some ten pages into *De Re Publica,* when she felt a gaze upon her. Looking up, she saw an older man, in his late forties or early fifties, looking at her with a slight smile on his face. She rapidly closed the book, curtsied, and said, "*Meester* Laurids?"

His smile expanded, as he waved her to sit. "Yes. And you are the Désirée of whom Alphons has spoken?" He crossed the room and sat in a chair opposite her, glancing at the book she had been reading. An eyebrow quirked. "Cicero?"

She flushed a bit, then responded. "Yes. I have always admired his acerbic wit."

Samuel Laurids let out a laugh. "Oh, yes, he is definitely acerbic! Have you read his *De Oratore*? It is a masterpiece!"

Désirée felt her lips pulling into a smile. "I have not had that pleasure, *Meester* Laurids."

Samuel smiled. "Oh you should, my dear. I have a copy here that I hope you will feel free to peruse." The smile slowly left his face. "But, if you are here, may I assume that you are in some difficulty?"

Désirée felt the side of her mouth sliding upwards. "That...would be accurate, *Meester* Laurids."

Samuel leaned back, almost certain that this was the woman Alphons had asked him to look out for. *Still....* "And would you, by chance, happen to have a note from Alphons on your person?"

She eyed him questioningly, but nodded, reaching into her skirt to pull out a piece of paper, and handed it to him. Samuel looked at it and smiled. There was a caret over the "o" in Alphons' name, a sign that this was real. He handed it back to her. "And what can I help you with, Désirée? Beyond," his eyes narrowed as he took in her appearance, "a bed, food, and, possibly, a doctor?"

She looked at him, and shook her head to clear it. "Those would, indeed, be welcome, but I have something that may be of import to Alphons and, possibly, you. May I give them to you?" At his nod, she handed him the four ledger books from her bag.

Samuel blinked. "And what, if I may ask, are these?"

Désirée looked at him and started to smile. "The last three years of accounts from *De Oprechte Mens*, a 'private club' owned by Geert de Zele."

Samuel's eyebrows were now augmenting his receding hairline. "Truly?!" He flicked the first book open and started to look, feeling his eyes widen as he read name after familiar name. Slowly, almost reverently, he closed the book, and looked at the young woman before him. "Allow me to show you to a guest room."

* * *

Samuel had spent the last two hours going over the books that Désirée had brought. If not a definitive guide, it certainly listed who had spent time with whom, and how much they had won, or lost, at the gaming tables. He gave a rather rueful smile at the simple entry of "Alphons, Désirée, three hours. No gaming.' *Three HOURS Alphons?* Samuel sighed. *It has been WAY too long since your wife died, my friend! Still*, he smiled a private little smile, *she seems to be a sprightly lass and, obviously, trusts you, else she would never have come here.*

The smile died from his lips as he considered the rest of the information in those books. *If de Zele had this, one can only assume that he used it to his advantage.* Samuel went back to the list of names he had compiled, and kept reading, punctuated by the occasional thought of *Him? Really?!?*

Baert Huis, Zandhoven

9:05 a.m.

Geert de Zele stared at the letter from Claes de Smedt in consternation. One line in particular caught his attention.

Questions are being asked, Geert, where you guaranteed that none would be. My sources tell me that they originate with one Alphons Verbannen. You need to get him off us. Now.

De Zele fumed at the audacity of de Smedt. *Who does he think he is?* Then his mind cleared and he started to focus. *Alphons? Yes, probably the same man. He will regret crossing me!*

De Oprechte Mens, Antwerp
12:05 p.m.

Lucretia sauntered into the office with a long-suffering smile on her face. *Every day, do the books.* She sighed, and sat down at the table, reaching behind her for the ledger. Which she couldn't feel. Twisting around, she saw that the last four ledgers were missing. She narrowed her eyes. *Hmm, Geert might take one, but not more. Where* are *they?* She rose and roamed through the office looking for the missing ledgers.

Finally, after several minutes of futile searching, she scanned the room once more. *Let's just make certain everyone is here.*

* * *

"Alright, girls, is everyone here?" Lucretia's voice sounded throughout the parlor. She scanned the crowd, then frowned. "Where are Albert and Désirée? Get them down here." She slitted her eyes. "*Now*!" Several people scrambled off, and Lucretia took a mug of broth and sipped it while she waited.

After a minute, Albert walked into the parlor, eyes shooting daggers at Lucretia. "Why did you wake me? I had to deal with that Frenchman last night, and I need my beauty sleep."

Lucretia stared at Albert. At eighteen, he was in his prime, and in great demand. Unfortunately, he knew it. "Shut your mouth, bitch. When I say to get your ass down here, I mean it." Her eyes slitted, "And if you want to try and go against me, I'll suggest that Geert *entertain* you for the next month. *Comprende*?"

The blood drained from Albert's face. "Of course, Lucretia."

She looked at him with an expression that said "Next time, you're dead." He wilted, and Lucretia looked around again. "Where's Désirée?"

"She's not in her bedroom or anywhere else we can see, Lucretia," one of the girls said.

"Really?" Lucretia lowered her eyebrows. "Hmmm. Search the entire house. *Go*!"

Baert Huis, Zandhoven
3:25 p.m.

Geert. The last four account books are missing. I might have expected you to take one, but not all four, at least not without telling me. Désirée has also disappeared. I do not know if these two events are connected, but they may be.

De Zele's eyes narrowed and he found himself tamping down a huge surge of anger. He turned to the cubby holes behind him and extracted the notes he had gathered on Alphons Verbannen. *Yes, they spent time together, but only once.* He frowned in thought. *Could he have recruited Désirée? It doesn't seem likely, but....*

He skimmed through the notes: *Business interests in Antwerp, but no house. Wait, what's this?* One informant had mentioned that Alphons usually stayed at the house of one of his bankers, Samuel Laurids. De Zele's eyes narrowed. *That closed-purse, sanctimonious bastard?*

The door to de Zele's office opened and Dirk Baert wandered in. "I'm bored, Geert. Father has had me doing accounts and reading contracts for *hours*!"

The petulant look on Dirk's face was familiar to de Zele. "Well, I have to go into Antwerp on business. Why don't I tell your father you're coming with me and you can slip off to the Club? We can meet up there for a late supper."

Dirk's face lit up. "Wonderful! I just knew you would have an idea."

De Oprechte Mens, Antwerp

8:25 p.m.

I do love Antwerp, de Zele thought as he made his way to his office. *You can arrange almost anything with enough silver.* He spotted Lucretia talking with one of the girls and, upon catching her eye, jerked his head towards the office door, getting a nod in return. He went over to the sideboard and poured himself a glass of wine.

He had barely sat down when Lucretia entered, closing the door behind her. "I told the kitchen to hold dinner for you and Dirk. He's upstairs right now with both Albert *and* Theodore—greedy!"

De Zele smirked. "His greed is our profit, Lucretia." The smirk disappeared and was replaced by coldness. "Have you found the ledgers or Désirée?

"No." Her eyes slitted. "And when I do find Désirée, I doubt she will enjoy the experience."

De Zele gave her a razor-edged smile. "When we get her back, use her as you like. Just make sure to dispose of the body afterwards where it won't be found."

He leaned back with a satisfied smile on his lips. "I've made inquiries and hired a few men." He shrugged. "We don't really have anything solid, but I *might* have a clue as to where she is. I've set watchers on the house."

Between Antonio and Bastião's company areas, De Manrique's camp
Tuesday, July 15, 6:25 a.m.

When Antonio had returned the previous evening, he found a note from Bastião asking him to come to his camp at Prime. Against his better judgment—his head was still somewhat the worse for the copious quantities of wine from the night before—Antonio had dragged himself out of bed, dressed, and armed himself. He knew he was late, but *Christ Crucified, Bastião should be glad I'm there before Terce!*

He walked around a bend in the road, shaded by trees, and could just make out the entry to Bastião's camp when he spotted three soldiers walking towards him. "Excuse me, do you know where we can find Don Antonio de Godelleta?" the one in the middle asked.

Antonio nodded, then winced. "That's me. What do you want? Did you want to join the Marksman's League?"

"No sir, we have a message for you." The three men kept walking until they were only three feet away.

"Oh?" Antonio raised an eyebrow. "Well, what's the message?"

The man in the center twisted to his right and opened a courier bag, quickly turning back and slamming his right foot into Antonio's stomach. Antonio doubled over in pain and could feel the contents of his stomach flowing up through his throat and nostrils, splattering the ground before him. "Keep your fucking nose *out* of the affairs of your betters. This is your first, and last, warning."

Antonio felt the impact of another kick, this time to his lower ribs, and he heard a crunch. He fell to the ground and screamed as he was kicked again and again, while he tried to curl into a ball. Vaguely, he thought he heard shouts and a single shot. The blanket of darkness that wrapped around him was most welcome.

Verbannen Huis, Huldenberg
Thursday, July 17, 1631, 6:25 p.m.

Alphons had been awake and working on his report since well before Prime. He had just finished reading the latest dispatch from Samuel Laurids, smiling when he heard that Désirée was safe, and feeling awe that she had dared to steal the ledger books. Samuel's description of their contents, however, left him frowning. *The potential for blackmail and extortion is astounding!*

He looked up as one of the footmen knocked, then entered carrying a dispatch. "What is it, Jean-Marc?"

"It's from Don Antonio's camp, sir. The courier is in the kitchen, waiting to see if you have a reply."

Alphons nodded and held out his hand, taking the dispatch and opening it. "*Oh verdomde hel*!" He looked up. "Tell the courier I will have several responses for him, probably in half an hour. Make sure he has a good meal." Jean-Marc nodded and left. Alphons returned to the dispatch, sent by one of Antonio's friends, skipping the rather verbose introduction.

No one seems to know how to contact Antonio's family but, since you two seem to be so friendly, we thought you might. He is in pretty rough shape—several broken ribs, a broken arm, and an astonishing number of bruises. He almost looks like a Blackamoor! And he has not woken up yet, which is worrying everyone.

No one seems to know who did it, but that Bastião fellow seems to think it was ordered by some quartermaster general, though I cannot see why that would be. Anyway, listen, be a good fellow and contact his family if you can and let them know he should be as good as new in a couple of months, at least according to our horse doctor.

Alphons pulled out several pieces of paper, quickly sharpened his quill, and began to write.

De Oprechte Mens, Antwerp
8:15 p.m.

"Message for you, Geert," Lucretia walked into the office and handed de Zele a folded note.

Opening it quickly, he scanned it and started to smile. Grabbing a sheet of paper, he wrote quickly, sanded it, folded it, and handed it to Lucretia. "Here's the response." She took it and started to turn away. "Oh, and Lucretia? Start sharpening your knives." They shared matching grins.

Office of the Inspector General, Army of Flanders, Brussels
9:05 p.m.

Pedro entered Don Luis' office and quietly closed the door behind him. He walked over and handed Don Luis a thick dispatch. "From *Meester* Alphons Verbannen, Don Luis."

Don Luis raised an eyebrow, then opened the dispatch and started to read. Pedro had known Don Luis all his life, and shared a special bond with him. They were, after all, milk brothers—Pedro's mother had been Don Luis' wet nurse—so he recognized the gathering storm in Don Luis' expression. Quietly, he went over to the sideboard and poured a glass of xérès, placing it next to Don Luis' hand. "Make certain the door is locked, and pour one for yourself." He returned to reading, while Pedro smiled quietly and served himself, sitting down opposite Don Luis.

Finally, after several minutes, Don Luis looked up. His eyes were entirely black, with no distinction between the pupil and the iris. *That is NOT a good sign,* Pedro thought to himself.

"Do you know, Pedro, I don't think I have been this angry since I came here." The tone was calm, but the calm of unruffled water over a deep current.

"What has occurred, Don Luis?"

"It appears that Don Antonio has been assaulted—beaten—and is currently unconscious. Possibly on the orders of one of de Manrique's quartermasters general. Furthermore, *Meester* Alphons Verbannen and Don Antonio have discovered a rather far-reaching scheme to defraud our soldiers, probably aided and abetted by that same quartermaster general." He took a controlled sip of his xérès.

Pedro nodded, sipping his own xérès, letting the silence stretch. "Does he have any particular recommendations, Don Luis?"

A smile slowly appeared, more related to a shark than a grin. "Do you know, Pedro, he does. And I am inclined to act on them. Hmmm," Don Luis furrowed his brow, then started to nod. "Pedro, go and tell that courier to carry a message to *Meester* Verbannen that he is to meet us tomorrow evening in Kontich. And alert our runners; I will have more orders to go out as soon as I have written them."

Pedro started to rise. "And, Pedro? You're coming with us." His eyes were still black. "Make certain that you bring your sword and pistols with you."

De Vier Broers Inn, Kontich, Flanders
Friday, July 18, 1631, 6:25 p.m.

Alphons walked into the inn, flanked by three of House Verbannen's footmen, all heavily armed. He had little difficulty recognizing Don Luis. *It's hard not to guess who he is when he's surrounded by armed retainers.* Walking over, he bowed and said, "Do I have the honor of speaking with Don Luis de Guevara y Zúñiga?" At a curt nod, he continued. "I hope that Your Excellency will pardon me for introducing myself. I am Alphons Verbannen."

Don Luis started to smile. "Meester Verbannen! Charmed to make your acquaintance, although I would have wished it was under better circumstances." His eyes flickered towards Verbannen's footmen, then back and to his left. "Pedro? Would you be good enough to show Meester Verbannen's men to the rooms we have for them?" Pedro nodded and rose, leading the footmen away.

"Please, sit down. Have something to drink. I believe our host will have something to eat soon." Alphons gave a short bow, slid a chair out, and sat. "So, Meester Verbannen, I read your missive with great interest."

Alphons had a rather crooked smile on his face. "Thank you, Your Excellency. But, if I might beg a favor?" At a raised eyebrow, he continued, "Every time I hear 'Meester Verbannen,' I look around expecting to see my father. Would it be possible for you to call me 'Alphons'? Or, if formality is essential, 'young Master Verbannen'?"

The smile on Don Luis' face stretched into a grin, before he broke out laughing. "Alphons it is, then. And please, call me Don Luis." The laughter faded from his face. "Alphons, you levied serious accusations in your missive." He waved a hand in negation. "I have no doubt that you are correct, and I have dispatched one of my assistants, along with a dozen cavalry troopers, to arrest that particular quartermaster general and his four clerks. After what happened to Don Antonio, I almost hope they resist. I have also sent another assistant to arrest de Smedt, and another for Baert."

Alphons briefly matched the feral grin on Don Luis' face. "Your assistant should reach de Manrique's camp tomorrow. How do you wish to proceed in the matter of de Zele?"

"De Zele?" Don Luis cocked his head. "I thought he was *Meester* Baert's general factotum."

"He is, but he is the one I believe is behind this scheme, not Adrienne Baert." Alphons' eyes grew cold. "He has, as far as I can tell, taken advantage of *Meester* Baert, and subverted his son, Dirk, into unwholesome pursuits."

Don Luis shrugged. "Surely, a Master is responsible for his employees? Should I not have him arrested as well?"

Alphons closed his eyes, let out a sigh, and let some of his pain show. "I am afraid that *Meester* Baert is...ah, becoming mentally infirm. His memory is failing, and he seems...clouded in his perceptions, as if he must work them out anew every time."

Don Luis winced, but nodded. "Yes, I have seen that before. It is as if God himself slowly withdraws our will and knowledge, making us like the flowers in the field who live only from moment to moment." He let out a sigh, then gathered his thoughts. "But you say the son is subverted? How so?"

Alphons nodded. "Yes, his eldest, Dirk. De Zele appears to have *encouraged* him in unwholesome habits. I saw as much when I visited his club in Antwerp." Alphons shivered. "It made my skin crawl. The younger son,

Luc, appears to be whole and of good character. I managed to talk with him for a few moments when I was last in Antwerp."

"Could the younger son—Luc?—manage the business?"

"Probably, Don Luis. He might need some support, but he could grow into it easily enough."

Don Luis nodded and thought. "So, how would you suggest we deal with de Zele?"

"The rack and hot irons?" Alphons said in a playful manner, before his face grew serious. "I have ample evidence that he is involved in extortion and blackmail, in addition to his other crimes. I have to wonder if he might be working for the Dutch, but I have no proof of that."

Don Luis started to nod. It was certainly plausible; more than enough for him to issue, and serve, a warrant for arrest. "We will find out. My question, however, was of a more tactical nature."

It was Alphons' turn to nod. "I would suggest that we ride into Antwerp as early as possible and go immediately to my banker." Seeing a questioning look, he continued. "*Meester* Laurids has been monitoring de Zele, as well as collecting information on him at my behest. He should know exactly where we can find him."

Don Luis started to smile. "Excellent. Then we arrest him."

Laurids Huis, Antwerp
Saturday, July 19, 1631, 3:15 a.m.

Six men moved through the front door of Laurids *Huis*, the final one closing the door just as the waning moon appeared from behind clouds. Two of them bound and gagged the unconscious doorman, while three started carefully up the stairway to the second floor. The fourth moved into the library, uncovering a lantern, and proceeded to search the room. *It's amazing how much information a kitchen boy will tell a friendly barmaid,* their leader thought with a smile. The target was in a guest room at the rear of the second floor, and should be well asleep.

Moving almost silently, they came to the target's door and slowly eased it open. Three of them drifted into the room, while two remained outside the door watching with drawn pistols. A few slight, muffled sounds came from the room before the door opened again and the leader came out, signaling for one of the door guards to move back to the stairs. Soon, two more men appeared, carrying a bound and gagged body between them.

The group flowed down the stairs meeting up with the searcher, who shook his head. They were approaching the front door when the body arched and lashed out with bound feet, knocking over a vase that smashed to the floor with a heroic noise. The leader hissed "*Verdorie*!" Pointing at the two pistoleers, he whispered, "You two, cover our retreat. Run for it in a minute. The rest of you, knock the bitch out and let's get out of here."

A cry rang out from the second floor. "What's going on?" A man holding a cudgel dashed out of the back of the house. A pistol shot rang out, and the cudgel wielder screamed and was thrown backwards, writhing on the ground. The shooter turned and ran while his partner walked slowly backwards, pistol moving side to side. Lights started to blossom as he reached the door, turned, and ran.

The basement of De Oprechte Mens, Antwerp

6:15 a.m.

Désirée was roused to consciousness by a bucket of cold water. She tried to move, but found that she was shackled, spreadeagled hanging three feet above the stone floor on some type of cross suspended by chains from the ceiling. Shaking her head to clear it of water, she saw Lucretia standing in front of her with a vicious smile on her face. "Welcome back, Désirée. I doubt you will enjoy your return, but I will."

* * *

Geert de Zele was upstairs in the office, trying to reach a decision. *They couldn't find the ledgers, even if they got the bitch. Someone, probably Laurids, will be coming after me and he still has enough evidence to get me hanged*. Finally, he sighed. *Oh, well, it was good while it lasted,* he thought as he gathered a number of papers, including letters of credit in a different name, and stuffed them into a courier bag. The papers were followed by all of the coins in the office. After a last glance around, he left, closing the door behind him.

Laurids Huis, Antwerp
7:30 a.m.

It was a large party that rode towards Laurids Huis, led by Alphons, who knew the way, and Don Luis. When they arrived, they could see comings and goings, including members of the town watch. Alphons frowned as he dismounted and walked up and into the house followed by Don Luis. Alphons, noting Samuel in the library talking with an officer of the watch, strode in that direction, with Don Luis a step behind. "What has happened here, Meester Laurids?"

Samuel looked up, said something to the watchman, and came over, giving Alphons a curt nod. "Alphons, and...?" he trailed off looking towards Don Luis.

"Don Luis, may I have the honor of presenting *Meester* Samuel Laurids?" Receiving a nod, he continued. "Don Luis, here is *Meester* Samuel Laurids, my banker, friend, and one who has been of immense aid in the current investigation. I commend him to you as an excellent and worthy man." Turning to Samuel, he said "Meester Laurids, here is Don Luis Phelipe Ladrón de Guevara y Zúñiga, the *Veedor General* of the Army of Flanders, who commissioned this investigation."

Samuel gave Don Luis a deep bow. "It is an honor to make your acquaintance, Veedor General."

A slight smile ghosted over Don Luis' lips, as he gave a small nod back. "Meester Laurids, Alphons has told me of your aid, and I appreciate it. Now, will you answer Alphons' question? I, too, wish to know what has happened here."

Samuel's face was stony as he responded. "Some four hours ago, my house was breached. My doorman was assaulted, my night guard was killed, and," he closed his eyes and took a deep breath, letting it out, "a guest in my house was abducted." He turned to Alphons "I am so sorry, Alphons, but they took Désirée."

Alphons blanched. "Who did this, Samuel?"

"I don't *know*, Alphons, but the only person I can think of would be de Zele. Whoever it was searched my library as well as kidnapping Désirée."

"Not your upstairs office?" Alphons cocked his head.

"No, just the public office area in the library."

Don Luis looked intrigued. "You have *two* offices, Meester Laurids?"

"Yes, Your Excellency." He gave a small smile. "I use the library as the public office. It contains nothing of a truly confidential nature, and all of its files are duplicated in my private office upstairs. Very few people know of my private office, and fewer still have ever been there."

"An interesting stratagem, Meester Laurids, and one I may adopt. I thank you for the idea." He frowned for a moment. "Alphons, I think it is time to pay a call on *Meester* de Zele. Do either of you know where he is now?"

Samuel cleared his throat. "As of last night, he was at *De Oprechte Mens*, Your Excellency. I cannot guarantee he is still there, but that is the latest information I have."

"Excellent. Then that is where we go next." Don Luis noticed Alphons loosening his sword, and checking his main-gauche. "Um, Alphons, with no disrespect intended, how well do you use those?" His hands flicked towards the heavy rapier and main-gauche.

Alphons started a small, cold smile. "My father had me trained as he was, Don Luis, and I have kept in practice."

De Oprechte Mens, Antwerp

7:55 a.m.

Don Luis had seconded the senior watch officer and half a dozen of his men. Together with the dozen cavalry, Alphons' three footmen, Samuel, and sundry others, it was a large group that pulled up in front of *De Oprechte Mens*. The senior watch officer led the way and tried to open the front door. "Locked, Your Excellency."

"Pedro! Organize the men and break this door down."

Alphons watched as Don Luis' servant, Pedro, tapped four men and handed them axes from his saddlebags. *Well, Don Luis appears to be prepared.* He continued watching as Pedro organized the men in an assault on the door which, within a minute, swung open.

Don Luis, Alphons, and the senior watch officer stepped inside, seeing a man skidding to a halt in front of them. "*Wel verdomme* are you doing? We're closed!"

Don Luis gave him a disdainful look as only a Spanish aristocrat can. "Watch your tongue, lest I have it from your head. Where is de Zele?"

The man sputtered for a moment, then responded. "Gone, Master. He left an hour ago."

"*Kijk Meester*, send a runner and order your men to try and detain him. You have his description." The officer nodded, and signaled one of his men.

Alphons stepped forward, rapier in hand. "Where is Désirée? I am certain that if you answer our questions quickly and accurately, His Excellency," he waved his left hand at Don Luis, "will have mercy on you." His eyes narrowed. "Of course, if you try to lie, or obstruct us, I suspect that he will be inclined to the opposite. Choose!" he barked out, watching the man deflate.

"Désirée is in the basement with Lucretia. She gave orders to be left alone." He turned to Don Luis, "And what questions can I answer for you, Your Excellency?"

Don Luis held up his hand, and looked over his shoulder "Meester Laurids? Of your goodness, attend me." Looking back at the now thoroughly cowered man, he said, "Show Meester Laurids to whatever office is here." He glanced around. "Pedro, assign two men to guard *Meester* Laurids."

Alphons was quivering and, to Don Luis' perception, ready to explode. He looked at the trembling man in front of him. "But first, show *Meester* Verbannen to the basement." Turning to Alphons, he said, "Take your men with you, Alphons."

Alphons nodded and signaled his men forward. "This way, Masters." The servant led them to the back and down a short flight of stairs, lit by an occasional lantern. He pointed at a stout door about twenty feet away. "That's Lucretia's *workroom*. It is probably locked and barred."

Alphons peered around in the lantern light, but saw nothing that could be used to open the door. "Jean-Marc, go upstairs and borrow the axes." Jean-Marc took off at a run, while Alphons looked at the trembling servant. "And what should I expect to see in there?"

"Nothing you would like, Master. Once Lucretia gets going, it can be...." his voice trailed off, but his face said it all.

Alphons tried to compose himself, but was afraid that he was failing. "Do you think Désirée is still alive?"

The man nodded his head vigorously. "Probably, Master. Lucretia likes to, ah, savor her projects, making them last for several days."

"And what does her *workroom* look like?"

The man paled. "I don't know, Master. No one who goes in there comes out alive except Lucretia. I swear by God's Holy Mother, that's the truth!"

* * *

Lucretia looked to the side as the pounding on the door started. *What the fuck? Who—? If Geert needed me, he would have rung the bell. Whoever it is will regret it!* She picked up her favorite whip and a long dagger. Looking at Désirée, she said "I'll be back soon, Dearie."

* * *

The door burst open to show a scene that might have been painted by Breugel in one of his darker moments. Torchlight illuminated the body of Désirée hanging in the air, suspended on a cross, while highlighting Lucretia, holding a whip and long dagger. Alphons stalked into the room, rapier and main-gauche at the ready. Lucretia's lip twisted as she lashed out with the whip, which wrapped around Alphons' right wrist and stripped away his rapier, sending it flying into the wall.

Alphons had never trained or practiced against a whip, but he knew the crucial rule about distance weapons: get inside them. Despite the pain screaming in his right arm and wrist, he launched himself forward into an acrobat's roll, dropping his main-gauche and coming up two feet in front of Lucretia, just in time to feel a dagger skid over the chainmail he wore under his clothing.

As he surged upwards, he grabbed first her crotch, and then her throat, lifting her up and then slamming her into the stone floor. As she screamed and her dagger skittered across the stone floor, Alphons dropped on her stomach with both knees and slapped her open-handed in the head, aiming for her ears. Despite the pain she was in, she tried to attack him with curved fingers, attempting to rake his face. Alphons grabbed her hands, twisted and heaved her upright even as he slammed his forehead into her face, hearing the crunch of her nose breaking. He felt her collapse.

Alphons looked up at his men, and gave a satisfied smile. None of them had ever seen Alphons fight hand to hand before, except for practices in the salle, and they seemed shocked. "Tie this bitch up, and get Désirée free and onto a stretcher. I need to talk with Don Luis."

* * *

Alphons walked into the office, seeing Don Luis and Samuel leaning over, examining ledger books. They glanced up at his entry. Samuel looked shocked. "Are you alright, Alphons?"

Alphons snorted. "Better than Lucretia who," he turned to Don Luis, "is now bound and waiting for you."

"And the girl?"

Alphons shook his head. "She is alive, Don Luis, but in bad shape, given how much blood she seems to have lost." Alphons glowered and his voice sank. "And how much skin seems to have been flayed from her." He flicked his eyes to Samuel. "Samuel, of your goodness, could you see that she has the best doctor available? And could you guest her until she recovers? I will cover all expenses and leave two of my men with you as security."

"No, *I* will cover any expenses. And security, if *Meester* Laurids will accept." Don Luis said. "She was instrumental in bringing this investigation to its conclusion. Her wounds, taken in *my* service, are *my* responsibility.

This is a matter of honor, and I will not be gainsaid." Samuel bowed acquiescence. "Good. Now, how long will it take to finish the investigation?"

"Maybe a week, Don Luis." Alphons glanced at Samuel, who nodded. "I will need to travel to de Manrique's camp and get some information from your assistant and from Don Antonio and then to de Smedt's house and see what your other assistant has turned up."

Don Luis thought about that, then nodded. "I will give you a letter of introduction so that they will release any information you want. Get that," he pointed at Alphons' right arm, "seen to before you leave, and I will see you in a week in Brussels. Oh, and send my best wishes for a speedy recovery to Don Antonio. I would like to see him come with you, but if he is not up to travel, I will understand."

Laurids Huis, Antwerp
Tuesday, July 22, 1631, 5:45 p.m.

There were times when Samuel Laurids felt like taking the Name of God in vain, and decoding this message was one of them. Thankfully, he had never had to encode a message in this particular cypher. Finally, after four hours of work, he managed to read the actual message. *An entire town appeared in a flash of light? They defeated a tercio near Badenburg?!? They have no established religion and have welcomed Jews?!?!?!* He leaned back in thought, before nodding slowly. *I must tell Alphons about this when he comes by tomorrow on his way to Brussels!*

Office of the Inspector General, Army of Flanders, Brussels

Saturday, July 26, 1631, 1:45 p.m.

"Don Antonio Manuel Miguel de Godelleta and Meester Alphons Verbannen, Veedor General."

Don Luis rose as he saw Alphons and Antonio walk through the door, his eyes widening as he took in the fading bruises on Antonio's face, immobilized left arm, and careful step. "Don Antonio! I am delighted to see you, but sit, sit!" He watched as Antonio made his slow way over to a chair, sitting with obvious relief. "Alphons, please, sit as well. Pedro, could we have a bottle of xérès and three glasses?"

Pedro was already by a sideboard, having opened a bottle and picked up three glasses. He carefully brought them over to the table, set them down, bowed and left. Don Luis poured and handed each of them a glass, taking the last for himself. "To Spain!" he toasted, and the others echoed him.

Settling his glass on the table, he leaned forward. "Don Antonio, I am delighted to see you up and about. I had feared that you would be unable to attend."

Antonio smiled wryly. "Alphons only let me come on the condition that I use a sedan chair."

At the flicked glance from Don Luis to Alphons, the latter nodded. "It took us two days to get from Antwerp to Huldenberg. After the first day, when Don Antonio tried to ride, I ordered a sedan chair." His lips twitched. "I didn't want him falling out of the saddle and doing himself further mischief."

Don Luis had a genial grin on his face. "An excellent choice, Alphons. I can't have one of my best investigators incapacitated. And you," he turned to Antonio with a mock frown, "heal up quickly, even if it means you have to take a sedan chair!" Turning back to Alphons, he asked "Do you have the final report?"

Alphons waggled a hand. "As much of one as we can do now."

Alphons reached into a dispatch bag and pulled out a thick wad of paper, handing it to Don Luis, who looked at it, then said, "Summarize, please. I can read the details later."

Alphons nodded. "De Zele appears to have been the mind behind this entire operation, at least from what we can tell from his records. He received kickbacks from de Smedt, Vizard, and the quartermaster general, to the tune of over fifty thousand guilders during the past three years. Probably more, but that's what we have documented."

Don Luis nodded, and Alphons continued. "Luc Baert has taken over his father's business, and has cooperated in every way with your assistant. His brother, Dirk, well, I hope you don't mind that I used your name?" Don Luis' faint smile became predatory, and he slowly waved his hand in a tell-me-more gesture. "I told Dirk that he had two choices: join a monastery and forswear all claims to his father's business, or face charges from the Church and civic authorities for his...venery. He chose the former, signed the papers and entered a Benedictine monastery."

"A masterful solution, Alphons." The grin slowly faded. "And the others?"

Alphons stifled a smile. "My father has been in contact with a number of people he knows and trusts. I have included a list of them in the report. He has also been *mentioning* certain facts to them, and believes that they will be able to provide all of General de Manrique's requirements in a timely manner and with quality goods." *And father will get a finder's fee for every contract.* "He did suggest that de Smedt be charged and fined."

Don Luis nodded. "As he should be. I suspect that he will be lucky if he has enough money to sell sausages on the street after we are finished with him." His eyes grew cold. "If he lives." He shook his head and snorted. "Alphons, would you be willing to keep an eye on these new suppliers?"

Alphons looked a little out of sorts. "In almost any circumstances, Don Luis, I would agree. Unfortunately, my father is determined to send me on a trade mission, which will keep me from Flanders for some time." He coughed, then looked Don Luis in the eyes. "That said, I am certain that my father would be happy to keep an eye on them while I am gone."

Don Luis cocked his head. "A 'trade mission'?"

"Yes, Your Excellency. I am being dispatched to Thuringia to explore new opportunities."

"In Thuringia? I would not have expected any new opportunities thereabouts, what with the aftermath of Tilly's capture of Magdeburg!" Don Luis exclaimed.

Alphons nodded. "That very disruption has shifted patterns of trade, and my father believes that we need to know how." He shrugged. "It may be of benefit to many of the Catholic polities: Flanders, Cologne, the Rhineland, Franconia."

Don Luis frowned, then shrugged. "I am certain that your father has his reasons. I would welcome his oversight of these new suppliers, and I wish you a safe, and prosperous, journey. Now, let us talk about...."

* * *

A few minutes after Antonio and Alphons left, Pedro entered the room and closed the door, quickly moving to collect the glasses. "You might as well grab a glass and join me, Pedro. I'm sure you have some questions."

Pedro chuckled as he took a glass, sat down, and poured some xérès. "You might say that, Don Luis. I can understand why you are cultivating Don Antonio; he is a good agent and has excellent contacts. I am less sure as to why you want to cultivate his cousin."

Don Luis nodded and sipped his own xérès before placing it on the table. "Did I ever mention that I met Don Antonio's grandfather?" At Pedro's shaken head, he continued. "He was a man of unimpeachable honor. Nothing was more important to him than that he should be perceived as 'honorable', a viewpoint inherited by his eldest son. And, as we both know," a wry grin appeared on his face, "the outward appearance of honor can be costly, especially for those houses whose fortunes have not flourished."

Pedro let out a snort, then sipped his xérès, waiting for Don Luis to continue. "Don Raul as he was, *Meester* Raul Verbannen today, felt that honor was best served in the husbanding of resources and the careful cultivation of wealth, even at the expense of that outward appearance of honor. Finally, after several years, Don Raul was asked to leave to save the family from further 'embarrassment.' He came here and, over the past forty years, has built up an extensive network. To this day, he still sends his brother support for the betterment of the people on their estates."

Pedro nodded. "So I understand. Still, Don Antonio has access, so why cultivate either of the *Meesters* Verbannen?"

Luis smiled. "Simple, Raul. Don Antonio is honorable and, as you note, a good agent. But he has a, shall we say, 'limited scope' where honor is concerned; his grandfather's influence no doubt. *Meester* Verbannen, on the other hand, has a much more expansive understanding of honor as, I believe, does his son Alphons." He leaned forward. "And Raul, we will need that in the years to come."

Something New

Bethanne Kim

Grossliebringen, West Virginia County
March 1633

Snap! Johan jumped back and Sibylle giggled.

Snap! Sibylle stumbled back, knocking a basket of mending to the floor as Johan snickered.

Sibylle crossed her arms, glaring in the general direction the towel had come from. "Mutti!"

Smug, Else Müllerin's eyes remained focused on her first-born child. "You shouldn't have laughed, Sibylle, you know what a serious matter this is. And you, Johan, need to get betrothed. You've turned down every suggestion anyone, including your master, has made. It's high time you started thinking about your masterwork and opening your own bakery. You know you need a wife for that, Ring of Fire or no Ring of Fire."

He pouted. "I've met every girl you asked me to. It's not my fault they are all so awful. The last one had to write down the numbers to figure out how much three items would cost! What kind of wife would she make?"

Else sighed, sitting down on a chair and motioning her headstrong eldest to do the same. "That's fair enough about Lysistra. What kind of name is that for a German girl, anyway? If I'm being honest, I'm fairly certain Master Deckert only introduced you because his wife's family has been pushing her to find the young woman a husband with prospects."

Hands cupped on the table in front of him, Johan looked up. "So, what's your point? Why are you bugging me again if you're admitting you can't find anyone? Why can't I just have Sibylle help me until I find a wife?"

Eyes bugging out, Sibylle barely restrained herself from answering until their mother did. Snap. "Stop being a child. Yes, she could help you now, but her vision is worse every year. How long until she can't read the account ledger or even check deliveries to be certain you aren't being shorted?"

Eyes downcast, Sibylle's voice was almost lost in the sounds of the busy street outside. "Already, I can't truly see well enough. I can't tell if someone tries to steal something small from a store. And some of the merchants write so small I can't read it. Or they use watered-down ink to make it last longer, and it's too faint." Looking him straight in the eye, she concluded, "Johan, I really wish I could help, but we both know I can't."

Their *mutti*'s surprisingly young laugh surprised them both. "When God closes a door, he opens a window, *meine Kinder*. Haven't you noticed how the young up-timer woman, Krystal, looks at you, Johan? You know they view marriage very differently than we do. They let young people make the decision with no guidance from their families! From what I've seen, there is no thought given at all to business prospects when marriages are... Hmmm. Arranged is clearly the wrong word. Agreed? Close enough. When marriages are agreed."

Skeptical, Johan took a moment to think. "She only comes here to talk about medicine and helping Sibylle see better. How can she help me run a bakery?"

Else shook her head. "Silly boy. She doesn't have to. She's been coming here for quite a while now. Haven't you been listening? She owns a house in Grantville, or will soon enough, *and* she owns a house in Magdeburg. Do you think a woman who owns two houses and has enough money for a job like 'nurse' doesn't have enough to pay for help in a bakery?"

She raised her eyebrows, opening her eyes extra wide as she continued to stare at her eldest. "Well?"

Johan gulped.

"Boy, I've seen you look at her. Do not tell me you find her unattractive. And we've all heard your conversations, so I know you find her pleasant to be around. You do not have any reason to avoid at least considering a betrothal to her."

Johan gulped again, looked past his *mutti* to his sister, who was grinning like a maniac, gulped again, then nodded. "Yes, ma'am. I'll think about it." With that, he bolted from the house.

Deckert's Bakery

Johan had finished working for the day, but going back to the bakery seemed like the best way to avoid the machinations of his mother and possibly his sister, even though it meant going through quite a downpour. He pushed the door open, surprised by the tinkle of a small bell and a delighted laugh. "Frau Kyferin?"

"Don't look so surprised. I do live here. The new bell is most delightful, no? You, on the other hand, live with your family and have finished work for the day, so why are you here? Did you finally decide to get started on your master work?"

A red flush started at Johan's neckline, but mercifully didn't go far. "No, ma'am. I mean, yes, ma'am, the bell is delightful, but no, ma'am, I am not working on my master work just yet. But I did want to try that sourdough bread again. I'm not sure what I'm doing wrong, but the crust isn't quite crisp enough."

Hette Kyferin was dusting her husband's bakery as she did every day after closing, tidying up anything out of place. Johan and the other journeymen and apprentices who had worked in the shop over the years all knew it was her preferred approach to get them to open up and tell her something. "Is that so, Johan? Well, good luck with it. That lovely young up-timer girl—Kristine, was it?—she didn't stop by today like she usually does. I put aside some *brötchen* for her, and it's still there, waiting for Kristine."

"Krystal." The red moved a bit higher up, nearly to the top of his neck now. "Do you..." He trailed off, not wanting to seem interested.

"Do I know where she is? Of course. I'll be happy to take over some of the sourdough for you when you finish, or I can just take the *brötchen*. Either way, I'm waiting for the rain to slow down a bit. Just call out when it's ready, and I'll take it over to the Red Shield for you."

As the flush continued to creep toward his hairline, Johan fled for the kitchen and the dough he had left rising at the end of the day. *Perfect!* He took the final step of scoring it before baking, hoping this would be a perfect loaf of sourdough. *I can make Mutti a loaf another day. If the von up-time girl really is interested like they say, I don't want to waste this chance and get stuck with someone like Lysistra.* He shuddered, then slid the bread into the waiting oven before turning to clean up the small mess he had made.

* * *

Reichard Deckert was looking out the window at the main street when his wife, Hette, bumped his shoulder and slid an arm around his waist. Twisting his head, he saw her grin. "And why are you so pleased with yourself? It's just a small bell on the door."

"Not the bell, you goose. It's Johan." Reichard motioned her to go on. "And Krystal."

His eyes narrowed slightly. "As much as we all wish there was a 'Johan and' some female of marriageable age, I wasn't aware there was a 'Johan and Krystal.' Do either of *them* know there is a 'Johan and Krystal?'"

Hette snorted. "Not likely. Well, maybe Johan is getting an idea. I'll explain. You saw the sourdough he set out before he went home at the end of the day. He came back to finish it. I mentioned that Kristine, the up-timer, likes sourdough and didn't stop in for the *brötchen* I set aside for her. He corrected me on her name and blushed. Then I told him I could take some of his sourdough to her at the Red Shield along with the *brötchen* and he blushed more. And just now, after he put his bread into the oven, he walked over to give her the *brötchen* himself. I'll be quite surprised if he doesn't take the sourdough over when it's done."

Reichard craned his head to look toward the Red Shield, just a bit out of his view. "Hmm. Can't see him headed back yet, so he didn't just drop it and race back. You just might have a point there, woman." He spun around and pulled her in front of him, nuzzling her neck. "I don't know how you did that, but I'll take it! That boy has been too stubborn about finding a bride."

"I told you having him talk to Lysistra was a good idea."

"Yeah, desperation will make a man rethink how picky he's being. You know I wouldn't have let him go through with it, even if he had agreed, right?"

"Oh, honey, I wouldn't either. That girl needs to go to a convent. She's not smart enough to get married to any man who could earn an honest living. No decent hard-working man could afford a woman with so few practical skills. Speaking of practical, it is time for us to enjoy our dinner."

Reichard twitched the curtains closed and admired the view between the front windows and the dining table.

* * *

His clothing and hair just starting to dry from the heat of the oven, Johan grabbed the basket of *brötchen* and rushed out the door toward the Red Shield Inn before he could talk himself out of it. Sprinting down the street, he swung into the entrance and stopped in the doorway, mortified that he was now slightly spattered with mud and hadn't even taken the time to wipe the bits of flour off himself. *This isn't the best way to make a good impression.*

As he looked across the room, he spotted Krystal spilling the house special stew down her front and swearing like a sailor, as the up-timers would say. *She might be as messy as I am.* Unfortunately, he grinned just as she looked over at him. "Fräulein! I didn't mean any insult!" All he could do was stare after her as she raced up the stairs.

Shoulders drooping, he looked around, hoping for an answer, when her friend from Red Shield, Ursula Durer, walked up, smiling. "*Guten Tag*, Johan. Would you like me to give those to Krystal when she comes downstairs? It shouldn't be long. I think she is just washing her hands."

Johan nodded, holding out a basket. "'Please, can you give this to Fräulein Krystal? I did not mean to upset her. When you visit Grossliebringen, she comes in to have a roll at the bakery where I work but today it is so rainy and she did not come in, so when Master Deckert told me she came to the inn, I brought *brötchen* here for her." *Nein! The Mistress. She won't know the difference. It's okay.* He took a deep, steadying breath in and blew it out. "I must go back. I have more bread in the oven. I am sorry I cannot stay to give it to her myself."

Peeking into the basket, Ursula snagged a roll for herself. "I'm sure Krystal won't mind if I eat just one." She wiggled an eyebrow. "She does always seem to look for an excuse to stop in the bakery here. Odd that doesn't happen in other towns, isn't it? Almost like it's not the baked goods she's interested in."

Gulping hard, Johan fled home.

May

Reichard tore a piece from the new-style bread Johan had been working on for the past six weeks. Johan had gone to Grantville in search of a recipe worthy of being his masterwork and came back with...this. It was certainly different. He had watched Johan studying the recipes and instructions he brought back, working on his technique. Rolling and folding, and rolling and folding, and rolling and folding some more. This was the first time Johan had looked hopeful when he pulled the bread from the oven.

The bread was soft, the layers of golden flakiness clear once it was broken. "What is this, Johan?"

Smiling, some of the tension he had been carrying easing, Johan wiped a crumb from the corner of his mouth. "A croissant. Up-time, it was considered French, thus the name. I was thinking of giving it a German name, but perhaps it is better to use the English and call it a crescent roll." Reaching around the table, Johan pulled butter toward them. "It's even better with butter."

"And what isn't better with butter, my lad?" asked Reichard as he buttered the roll. Taking a bite, his eyes opened wider. "You're right, this really *is* better with butter. I think you have found your master work, my boy."

"Truly?" He let out a sigh that sounded like it went the whole way down to his toes. "I have more work, but that is a relief."

June

Ursula stopped in the bakery. "Half a dozen *brötchen*, please."

Hearing Ursula, Johan poked his head out of the back, looked around, then went back.

"What's up with him?"

Hette snorted but answered quietly. "Don't you play dumb with me. He was looking for Krystal and you know it. Is she in town today?"

"And why are *you* looking for Krystal?"

"Same reason you came over here for rolls, even though Renata already has perfectly good ones I dropped off this morning. Trying to get the two of them together. Now, is she here today?"

"Why else would I be here for *brötchen*? We are dropping off a dartboard we promised Renata and Francois for the inn. Well, more like Krystal just ran over them with words until they agreed to take one, but it's here now and she's getting ready to show people how to 'throw darts' to play the game. She even brought up having the bakers come over and try a game."

The two women exchanged the kind of glance that had struck fear into the hearts of many men throughout history. They were clearly plotting...something.

Hette nodded. "I'll send the journeymen over in five minutes. Apprentices too, if they are caught up on their work."

"Better make it fifteen. Give her a chance to get warmed up teaching."

As Ursula walked out the front door, Hette was walking into the back room.

* * *

Sibylle whacked her brother upside the head. "You." Whack. "Will."

Johan grabbed her wrist, stopping the motion before she made contact again. "Got it. I will go over to the Red Shield and try this new game. But I did not go earlier *because I was working*. You all wish for me to marry and become a master so much, and my work is part of becoming a master." When Sibylle gave a curt nod, he dropped her hand. "Good. Now, go home and tell Mutti I'm being a good little boy and trying to find a wife like everyone wants."

Hurrying, he caught up to the other journeymen on the street. When they entered the inn, he tried not to stare at Krystal, but the up-timers really were different. *She couldn't blend in no matter what she tried.*

Ursula bustled up to him. "Johan! Happy to see you all here. Don't be shy. Krystal offered to help anyone who wants to improve their form, and Ragndid has shown how much she can help. You can see that Hans has already taken her up on it. You don't want to hurt her feelings by not letting her help you, do you?"

Blushing again, Johan dipped his head and said, "When you put it that way, I guess I could go next." When Hans returned to his seat, Johan walked up. " Fräulein Krystal, *bitte hilfe mir.* I mean, please help me to learn this game."

Krystal stood to Johan's side, observing for a moment before adjusting his hand position. *Her hands are so smooth. I feel no callouses.* Lost in the moment, Johan's throw barely hit the dartboard. Frowning slightly, Krystal moved behind him. He started to turn, only to feel her hands firmly on his hips, trying to change his stance slightly. He relaxed, letting her move his whole frame into the position she thought best. His next throw was better, but there was room for improvement.

Glancing to the side, he saw his buddies grinning and winking as they toasted him with beer. He managed to keep from blushing until Krystal started sliding her hand down his entire arm, moving every muscle into the position she wanted, not just his fingers. Judging from the time she spent touching, but not moving, his biceps, she apparently appreciated the strength his years of baking had endowed them with.

* * *

As the dinner rush ended, Reichard, Hette, Else, and Lorenz were each nursing a beer as they watched the activity around the dartboard. Else nudged Lorenz. "See! I told you the von up-time girl liked our Johan." He grunted softly in reply.

Reichard nodded. "Aye, there seems no doubt she's interested in him, and these up-timers are odd about marriage. They act as if someone nineteen should make this kind of decision with no help from those more experienced in life." He sniffed, clearly offended by the idea. "Hette found out that Krystal brought him a croissant recipe. That's what gave him the idea of working to master those."

Lorenz raised an eyebrow. "Indeed? Interesting that he failed to mention that to his mother and me." Else nodded, her own eyebrows arched in surprise. "I hope these up-timers haven't given him too many foolish 'modern' notions."

Else patted her arm. "Don't worry too much. Ursula and I talk when they visit, and she's been advising Krystal. We'll certainly need to accept things being done differently with her, but is it such a bad thing if they spend some time together on these 'dates' before becoming betrothed? Perhaps if he had spent time with some of the other young women, he might have found a reason to like one of them."

Seeing her husband's yawn, Hette gathered her skirts, preparing to rise. "These young ones may be able to stay up late and still be ready for work when the ovens need to be fired and the dough mixed in a few hours, but we are not young anymore. So, I would like to go home now with my husband, who is much loved despite not being one of these 'love matches' the up-timers insist on. I bid you good night."

August

"Sibylle, I really think you should visit Grantville. You can get glasses so you can see!"

"Again, Krystal, I don't have the money for glasses."

"Again, Sibylle, I will find a way to help you."

Both women were clearly frustrated. This was obviously not the first time they had gone over this. Ursula was not willing to listen to it *again*. "Krystal, I left the anatomy book you wanted to show Sibylle with the horses. Do you mind getting it for me?"

Krystal snorted. "You know those horses hate me."

"Actually, it's just the gray who hates you. You, on the other hand, hate them both. Johan, can you help her? It's in the left saddlebag of the gray."

Once Krystal was out of the room, Ursula turned to Sibylle. "Stop arguing about it. No. This is not a conversation, Sibylle. I live in Grantville, you don't. They will find a way to get you the glasses and you will be able to see again, as long as you are wearing the glasses. It will change your life. Just accept it. Argue a bit more, if you must, but accept it and make a plan for when you think you can come to Grantville for a while and get the glasses. This is really not open for discussion right now because I don't know about you, but I want to see what Krystal and Johan are up to."

Krystal was checking out Johan who was stroking the gray because he really did love horses, and the gray really wasn't the friendliest horse around. His biceps flexed impressively. As he poked around in the saddlebag, Krystal moved in just a little closer than she needed to.

Ursula crossed her arms and tapped her foot. "Now, that's frustrating. I can't see what they are doing. I'm looking at their backs."

"Yeah, I can't see what they are doing even when they're in the same room as me, so I get that."

Ursula hugged Sibylle. "Krystal is looking at him like he's meat and she hasn't eaten in a week. I couldn't see his face at all, but I'm pretty sure he was making sure she had something to look at. And they are standing closer than just-friends normally stand."

"All in all, that sounds good for everyone who is trying to get them together."

Ursula wrapped her arm around Sibylle. "Exactly."

November

Johan looked at his big sister, as always, wanting to protect her. "Last ask. You're sure you want to do this?"

Sibylle glared at him. "Yes, Johan, I am quite certain I would like to see again. There is no doubt in my mind that I want to go to Grantville and receive a pair of these miraculous glasses of theirs. Ursula has convinced me that her family truly welcomes us into their home while we get settled. If you ask me one more time while we are traveling, I will tell Ursula to throw you out of their home and send you back to our parents. Clear?"

Unaccustomed to such irritation from his sister, Johan swallowed hard and nodded. "Clear."

Two Days Later

Standing on Market Street in front of the bakery he was working at while staying in Grantville, Johan rolled his neck, stretched his shoulders, and finally cracked his knuckles before stepping forward to knock lightly on the door. It was time for him to start work, but people in the apartments over the shops would still be sound asleep.

One of the apprentices opened the door. "Next time just come in. Use the back door. That's where we get deliveries from the train, and it's closer to the grocery store if we need something extra."

The hours flew by as he got used to his new workplace. As he was cleaning up for the day, he heard a familiar voice out front. Hurrying to finish, he grabbed two fresh *brötchen* and went out front. "Krystal? Why are you here?"

She grinned. "Afternoon snack. I still help my uncle at his pharmacy sometimes, and it's two doors down. Just across the railroad tracks. Hey! Fresh *brötchen* for me? You're the best!" She grabbed him by the arm. "You're done for the day, right? Everyone's cleaning up and you have your coat so I'm not taking no for an answer. We're going to get pizza at Marcantonio's, and you can't stop me. You also can't stop me from eating both these rolls. Sibylle's still at the eye doctor, so no trying to go get her and use that as an excuse. We're having a pizza date right now!"

Utterly bewildered and not actually wanting to say no to whatever a pizza date might be, Johan handed over the second *brötchen*, determined to roll with whatever Krystal had planned.

Grossliebringen, West Virginia
May 1634

Johan's face hurt. It actually hurt. He had taken Krystal on many dates and spent time with her family. It was going as well as his family and Master Deckert had hoped. Sibylle had glasses and settled into Grantville with a job and everything. And now, he had passed the exam and was a master baker.

His dreams were all within reach. He knew it was too soon to ask Krystal's family about a betrothal, because she had told him, "It's too soon—don't ask me to marry you yet." Not never, just not yet. So, he would be patient. But it was definitely moving in the right direction. Also, her aunt, his employer, had sat him down and discussed how up-timers thought about marriage. He was reasonably confident that was a good sign.

"Hi, Mutti! Vatti!"

Else almost bowled him over with her hug. "My son! The master baker." Her maternal pride was unmistakable.

His father's pride was every bit as clear, just a little less...energetic. "Son." The crisp nod and arm clasp conveyed more emotion than one might expect. "What now?"

"Um. Work?" He wasn't entirely sure how to answer.

"You know Master Deckert has to bring on a new journeyman since you aren't one anymore."

"It has been a long week. I brought some samples. Let's go inside and eat and talk. Please?"

Settling down at the kitchen table, he handed them each a bagel and cream cheese. "These bagels are a new thing from the up-timers. They opened a café selling them almost next door to the bakery where I was working. They said to come back next month and I can almost definitely have a job. It's a new shop, so they just need to be sure they have business, but it's next to the railroad station, so no one is really worried." He picked up a bagel, slicing it in half. "Here, people like them toasted, but you can eat them like this. Then spread on the cream cheese. Up-timers say they used to put it on quite thick, but it's hard to get so you should just use a small amount."

"Different."

"Chewy."

"This cream cheese. Is it made from cream?"

"Yes, that's why there isn't much of it. The up-timers love it. They even made cakes with it! But those are crazy expensive. They insist bagels are good with butter or jelly, or even made into a sandwich, but are best hot with cream cheese."

"And you might work at the place that makes these? So, you know how to bake them?"

Looking down at his hands, he shook his head. "No, I've tried but not mastered it yet." He looked his parents in the eyes, each in turn. "There is only one person who has truly mastered these bagels, and she will teach me. I have decided I wish to continue studying these new up-time breads."

Letting out a deep sigh, Else finished the last of her bagel. "And so, both of our children will live in Grantville. How are things with Krystal? Do you think you would be happy with her?"

"Yes, Mutti, I really do. It is too soon for a betrothal, but I have met her family. You must come to visit me and Sibylle. Krystal's Uncle Raymond said you can stay at his home so you can get acquainted. Perhaps next year, when she has graduated from nursing school, then perhaps she will agree to marry me. But you can have some conversations with her Uncle Raymond and Aunt Bethel to make some plans."

Lorenz looked at him, unmoving. "You've grown, son. You're a man now." He gave a sharp nod. "You will be a fine master with a fine shop, and a fine husband and father. This new path of yours, learning the up-time baking, if it is anything like everything else up-time, you will make a great deal of money from it, so we don't need to worry about you. But you must take care of your sister."

Johan shook his head. "I'll help Sibylle if she needs it, but I don't think she will. She has a good job and many friends. Don't tell her I said so, but she has even had a suitor or two interested in her. You can rest easy now. Your children won't be a burden in your old age."

Raymond and Bethel Little's Home, Grantville
December

Else and Lorenz stared up at the house in front of them. It had two towers and a massive green metal roof that covered nothing but an outdoor seating area. Johan cleared his throat. "It's not her house. We talked about this. Up-timer houses are different." He waved his hand, gesturing to cover the whole town. "There are more houses with porches like this than without. You know the plan. We talk to her aunt and uncle first, then we go talk to Krystal."

With a sharp nod, Lorenz put his arm out and walked up the concrete steps with Else. Not sparing a moment, he immediately knocked firmly on the door.

Bethel and Raymond Little both greeted them at the door, Bethel waved them inside as Raymond took their coats, gloves, and hats. As Else and Lorenz turned toward the living room, Bethel motioned them, instead, toward the dining room. "I don't know how much Johan has told you, but I don't think this conversation is going where you expect."

Pushing in his mother's seat, Johan spoke, "Don't worry. Mutti *und* Vatti, it's nothing bad. Just...different."

Lorenz looked at Raymond. "We came to speak about a betrothal. What is this nonsense about something 'different'?"

Lorenz's eyes narrowed as Bethel answered and Raymond sipped from the coffee mug in front of him. "We understand that up-timers are, well, rich"—her face quirked at that—"here and now, as uncomfortable as that makes us and as hard as it is for us to believe. Not to be rude, but there really isn't anything of value that Johan could give Krystal that she might possibly need."

Else put a restraining hand on Lorenz as he turned red and pointed toward his drink. "We have worried about this, yes, but thought an agreement had been reached before we took this trip here. Johan has been working for you and putting money aside."

Bethel nodded like a bobblehead. "Yes, he has! He's doing a great job with the bagels, and of course he makes great crescent rolls."

Johan broke in. "We're starting a new guild! It's going to focus on up-time breads, and I'm going to be the second master. Another baker from the bagel shop is going to be the first." He beamed.

Lorenz looked around. "And what has this to do with the betrothal?"

Raymond answered. "The betrothal gift. There is no *thing* Johan could buy her that she doesn't already have. But as an up-time baker, he can *make* her something from home, something you don't have here. Something that will bring her joy money cannot buy."

A bell rang and Johan and Bethel both headed for the kitchen. Lorenz stroked his beard and Else stared at a painting of Cinderella's Castle. A minute later, Johan slipped a plate in front of each of his parents as Bethel gave one to Raymond. "This is an American biscuit, and this is cornbread."

Lorenz's eyes opened wide as he tasted the biscuits. Before he could say anything, Johan poured gravy over another biscuit and motioned for his parents to try.

"That...is amazing. The biscuits with gravy are almost a meal. The first loaves of cornbread you tried were nothing like that."

Johan laughed. "Yeah, the first ones sucked. But are you okay with this? With my giving her breads that I have made, instead of, well, whatever you had in mind?"

Raymond nodded. "Krystal doesn't expect anything other than a ring, and it doesn't need to be an expensive ring. Just to show Johan's intention. She'll be thrilled with the biscuits and cornbread, which Bethel is pretty sure they've managed to keep secret from her."

Head resting on her husband's shoulder, Bethel agreed. "We just want to see Krystal and all the other kids happy like we are. And she really does want to marry Johan." She looked around the room. "If we're all in agreement, let's end the poor girl's suspense and walk over to her house."

July 1635

Stumbling a bit from his mother's firm push through the front door, Johan stopped in front of Bethel and Raymond. "I, um, was making my *mutti* crazy."

Bethel pointed to the empty chair in front of them. "Sit. Put her gift on the table. Breathe. Good, now let's talk about the new salt bagels and your idea for a pretzel bagel."

"Bagels? Now?"

Firmly. "Yes, now, because you are spiraling, and you know bagels. So, pretzel bagels?"

Ten minutes later, Johan was startled to hear Krystal's voice behind him. "Johan! This is a surprise. I planned to see you this afternoon, when I visit Sibylle. Why are you here?"

Raymond motioned toward the empty chair next to Johan. "He needed to talk to me and your Aunt Bethel. Since we expected you, we told him to hang out and wait for you." Johan looked decidedly on edge, the exact opposite of someone simply “hanging out”. He rather abruptly stood and handed her the box he had put on the table. When he moved it, a condensation mark was left behind. Since he still wasn't speaking, Raymond prodded him. "Go on, boy, talk to her. She won't bite."

"Your parents and grandparents remained up-time. Your great-grandparents died." The more Johan talked, the more confused Krystal became. "Your aunt and uncle are the closest adult relatives you have down-time, so I have spoken to them and asked them. Made certain they haven't changed their minds."

"Asked them...?" They had talked about it enough that she was sure she knew where this was headed but she needed him to say it. Realizing she might crush the box from Johan, she put it back down on the table.

Johan took the plunge. "Asked them permission to formally court you and to become betrothed. If you wish it. Do you wish it?" Krystal leapt into his arms and gave him a kiss that lasted long enough for Else and Lorenz to shoo her cousins away from the windows.

"I wish it! I definitely wish it!" She pulled back. "Your parents aren't being all weird about the betrothal gifts, are they?"

Lorenz used his gruffest voice. "We do have conditions." Everyone stood still, clearly not expecting this response. He grinned. "You must share! Open the gift now."

Inside she found a cheesecake with an engagement ring decoration on top.

"I also made biscuits, gravy, and cornbread, but those are in the oven to keep them warm."

Krystal squealed with glee, jumping on her new betrothed, then jumping down again and running for the kitchen. "I'll share the rest of it, but the cheesecake is all mine!"

A Shocking Development

Jack Carroll

Coudenberg Palace Gardens, Brussels

Summer 1637

The patrol passed the end of a wall running along one side of the fish pond, and turned the corner. The sight that greeted them was far from normal.

A saddled horse stood half across the path bordering the water, with its head down among the vegetables in the kitchen garden. While his comrades were still taking in that sight, it was the youngest guard, Esquivel Sanchez, who turned at the sound of a ripple to see a booted lower leg stretched out of the water to rest awkwardly on the bank. "Cabo, look!"

Cabo Ladron Garcia's response was commendably quick, as befitted one who had survived half a dozen battles. He was already pivoting toward the sight, shouting, "Pull him out!"

With three strong men hauling, barely a moment passed before the victim was out of the water and deposited on the path.

It proved to be Adriano Navarro. In Garcia's opinion, this was not good. Any misfortune befalling a courtier of Navarro's prominence was liable to have unforeseeable consequences, none of them likely to be advantageous to anyone, particularly three obscure palace guards. And Navarro was not moving.

Water rescue not being among the many skills common to Spanish soldiers, there was one obvious thing to do. "We must bring him to Doctor Loosens. Help me lay him across the saddle."

Throwing the patient face-down over the saddle accomplished one thing. Some water drained out of his mouth as the party double-timed up-slope toward the nearest door of the palace. Garcia wondered in passing how a cavalier of Navarro's grace and skill could possibly have been thrown from a horse, but sometimes strange things just happened. If there had been foul play, it wasn't apparent. His concern at the moment, however, was to hand this mess off to someone in a position to deal with it.

As the three of them carried Navarro inside, Garcia called on one other of his assets—a voice that had been heard more than once amid the chaos of a battlefield. "DOCTOR LOOSENS TO THE CLINIC! AT THE RUN! PASS THE WORD!'

Thirty or so paces down the corridor, a bearded face looked out of a doorway: Doctor Claeys Loosens himself. "What is the uproar for? Oh, I see. Bring him in." He drew back inside, and for a moment there were sounds of things being moved.

As they carried Navarro through the doorway, dripping all the way, Loosens pointed to a bowl on the floor and ordered, "Hold him with his face over that for a moment." The doctor stepped in between two of the rescuers, joined his fists under the patient's chest, and pulled up hard. A little more water sprayed out into the bowl. A couple more thrusts producing nothing more, the doctor ordered, "Get him up on the examination table." He was already pulling an affair of leather tubes off his shoulders and sticking the ends in his ears. He applied the opposite end to the patient's chest, and frowned. "This is not good. Jan, bring the electrocardiograph and the defibrillator, then begin breathing for the patient."

Garcia looked up and took in his surroundings for the first time. Unlike much of the palace, there was nothing ornate about this room. It was fairly generous in size, with a desk and a few chairs. The walls were plain white, and the floor was tiled. Shelves and drawers lined two of the walls.

An assistant Garcia had not paid any attention to, up to that point, pushed a wheeled stand up beside the examination table, then turned to a shelf at the back of the room to snatch up a pair of varnished wooden boxes the length of a man's forearm, festooned with knobs and dials, and topped by coiled electrical wires. The words blazoned across the lower edge in a line of gold leaf meant no more to Garcia than anything else arrayed on their front surfaces—Nederlandse Consortium voor Elektronicaproductie.

Once the boxes had been set down where the doctor could reach them while attending the patient, the assistant snapped on a couple of toggles and stepped away to reach for yet another piece of apparatus, this one a leather bag a little larger than a man's fist, trailing a short leather tube. He finessed the tube into the patient's throat and began rhythmically squeezing the bag. Meanwhile the doctor was pulling the wires out one at a time and sticking them to various places on Navarro's body. In another moment he did something to one of the boxes, and a handspan-wide paper chart started to scroll out of it, bearing an enigmatic black line waggling irregularly from side to side. The doctor growled something under his breath, then looked up. "You men have done your duty. Thank you."

Garcia waved his gratitude at being freed of further responsibility and led his party out of the room. Behind him he heard the doctor's raised voice. "Charge to fifty joules and stand clear!"

Rescue Squad Garage, Grantville
June 1635

Gerald Hunsaker stepped down from the back of the open ambulance and set down a bulky piece of apparatus on its deck. "That's what a defibrillator from up-time looks like. You guys wanted to see one? I imagine it's anybody's guess what you could build now, though. If you could build anything to do the job, that is. What brought this on, anyway?"

John Grover turned his head toward Adraien van Karm and gestured with a raised hand. Adraien wasn't in a position to just call the shots at General Electronics, but he and his partner Willem de Wael were paying the salaries of two of the three electronics engineers responsible for the company's burst of progress on the military's vitally needed vacuum tubes. He was certainly someone to listen to.

The marine insurer put on the sort of brief smile he might have used at the start of a discussion with a ship owner and folded his hands above his belt. "I will explain. Two months ago, my Aunt Renske had an appointment with your famed Anne Jefferson to see what might be done for some of the aches that come with age. I accompanied her, since she can sometimes use a little help getting around the city. Just as we were leaving and stepped into the street, a thunderstorm was passing. A bolt struck so near us that I heard no gap between the flash and the crash. Renske collapsed without even a cry. I was barely able to get my hands on her to cushion the fall. I pulled her back inside.

"Mevrouw Jefferson's understanding of what had happened was instant. Without a word she pointed at the examination table. She took the stethoscope draped around her shoulders and listened for a few seconds. She said to her assistant, 'No respiration. Chaotic heart sounds. We'll try

CPR.' She didn't explain then, and I knew not to waste time asking. She began a rhythmic pressing on Renske's chest while the assistant took some small piece of apparatus from a drawer, inserted it between Renske's lips, and blew a breath through it every few seconds. That went on for fifteen minutes or more, pausing now and then to listen for a moment. After a while Mevrouw Jefferson was saying things like, 'Heart sounds, but irregular,' 'We'll keep trying,' and then, 'Starting to settle down.' Finally Renske opened her eyes. The doctor sat back, listening through the stethoscope. She blew out a long breath, and said, 'Boy, that was close. For a while I wasn't sure we could pull it off without a defibrillator.' Then she explained what had happened, and what they had done.

"Now, I am in the insurance business. I am always concerned with saving life and property. What happened may sound like something so rare that it could hardly ever happen in that way with help at hand, but electricity is coming to our country, and I have been warned of the dangers that it brings. Particularly if the installation is done carelessly, or it is used carelessly. And I have been told that when anesthesia must be given for surgery, the heart may sometimes be disturbed. So I desire that those who may be called on to aid such accident victims and patients may have these tools within reach."

John looked across the half-circle standing behind the ambulance, toward Andy Rogers from Grantville Radio Labs. Andy was an experienced ham, not an engineer, but he knew his way around vacuum-tube circuitry even better than John. His factory had built the transmitters that had been shipped to the USE and Venetian navies the month before. John snorted. "I bet I know what you're going to say."

"Yeah," Rogers replied "Rob te Winkel and I studied the manual for this here thing. It's called a manual defibrillator, but it's manual only in the sense that there are user controls on the front for a trained doctor or tech.

It's from 1992. The guys who designed it were all microcomputer-happy. There's all kinds of automation inside and cardiologist juju baked into software. The front panel controls just tell the microprocessor what to do. When we push the button, it doesn't fire the shock, it tells the microcomputer that everybody's hands are clear and it has permission to fire when it sees the spike in the chaotic waveform that we told it to watch for. Gerry says it works pretty good. A lot of the time it takes only one shock to get the heart to quit thrashing and settle down to doing its job. Maybe in fifty years we could copy it."

"What are you saying, then?" John asked. "There aren't the means to do it in our lifetimes?"

"No," drawled Rogers. "What I'm saying is we can probably build something like they had in 1940. I think. Maybe with a year or so of work. Rob thinks so too, but he says there are some parts in even a 1940 version that we don't know how to make yet, but we probably could figure something out. Remember that book on cardiology from 1940, that turned up in the Round Barn museum? They had electrocardiographs then, and defibrillators too. Just nothing like this. Building them with vacuum tubes and relays, they just built the bare power circuits and amplifiers that did the actual work. A naked defibrillator and EKG. Totally manual.

"I can handle most of the circuit design, except for that weird business with the right leg electrode. I can't figure what that does, except the EKG goes nuts if it's not connected. Maybe Rob can explain it. Anyway, I'm almost sure for every part that goes into something from back then, there's a company somewhere in Grantville or Schwarza that can make it, or can figure out how to make it inside of a year. Well, except maybe for the big capacitor. That might be a challenge. And what we could get for the EKG output by then is a mechanical strip chart recorder, like they used in 1970, not a graphic display like that thing there. I'd ask Kudzu Scientific

Instruments. We have to see what the heart is doing, to know when to deliver the shock."

John picked up his coffee cup from the ambulance's deck. "Gerry? Would that work for your crews?"

"Sure. If those guys back then could learn to use that gear, we can too."

John stood thinking for about ten seconds, cradling his cup in his hands. "All right. We need to decide whether we're going to go ahead with this. But if we do, I don't want anybody's time wasted on any half-baked ideas.

"I've managed a lot of projects over the years. Made all the classic mistakes, don't want to do it again. The first step is to write a proper specification to tell the engineers what the product has to do. Everything about it. It has to be complete and correct. We'll begin by getting together everybody who knows anything about what a defibrillator and an EKG are supposed to be, and write down all the requirements. And the engineers will be there too, to tell us what's possible. Day after tomorrow is probably as soon as the hospital people can come. Start thinking about it, okay?"

Magdeburg Memorial Hospital
A few weeks later

Doctor Vittorio di Benedetti caught up with a colleague from Uppsala at the second-floor nursing station. "You have seen the examination results from Meister Schöffler, Petter?"

"Ja. It is unfortunate. Under other circumstances something might be done, to at least give him some more time, but as it is, he is too fragile to consider operating. He would likely expire on the table."

"Perhaps, with what we have heard of the work at Grantville Radio Labs...?"

Petter shook his head. "Vittorio, we all wish for that, but they promise nothing in less than a year. How long can Schöffler last? Three weeks? Four? At the least, he needs a pacemaker. And how far off is that, a decade? No, what he really needs is a heart transplant. And when was that first done up-time?"

Vittorio gave a long sigh. "1967, if I remember right. With five times the world's population to draw on for the talent and I suppose a hundred times the wealth."

"Yes. Still beating in a perfusion machine a man could carry in his hands. But now? My friend, we are down to our last duty to the patient and his family. We must tell them the truth and not deceive them with false hopes."

"It is so." Vittorio looked down to the floor and closed one hand into a fist, then raised it again to smack his fist on the waist-high partition separating the nurse's station from the hallway. "And next year, and next decade, and next generation, we will do better."

Bill Porter's Office
Grantville Power Plant

The place was as clean as practical, but even with the best of intentions, it was impossible to completely keep coal dust from getting in. Bill swept off a visitor chair with a hand brush before gesturing Robrecht te Winkel to sit down and lay out his circuit sketches on the desk.

Bill stuck out his hand. "Hi! Glad to meet another engineer. Annie Decker called over here from American Electric Works and said I could probably help you more than she could. Whaddya got?"

"Some problems with magnetics, Mr. Porter. She's all right with regular AC power transformers, she's designed enough of them, but she says you have a lot more experience with high-frequency magnetics. We were trying to figure out how to get the core laminations thin enough that we could run them at high frequency and make the electrocardiograph's power transformer smaller. We need to bring down the interwinding capacitance so we can meet the leakage current requirement. That's a medical safety thing that wouldn't matter in radio gear. It looked like it would turn into a manufacturing nightmare if it could be done at all.

"And then there's this flyback inductor." He pointed to the schematic diagram of the defibrillator's high voltage section. "Andy Rogers and I studied the flyback circuit on a schematic of a tube TV set, and came up with this. It looks like a transformer, but it really isn't. She thinks you might have done something like this for the voice modulator at WVOL. A magnetic core with a gap in it?"

"Okay, yeah," Porter acknowledged. "Yeah, the AM broadcast band only goes down to 530 kilohertz. No way we could build the magnetics for that with laminated iron cores. One kilohertz is pushing it, even with layers a thousandth of an inch thick. We wasted a lot of time trying. We had to come up with a way to make powdered iron. Even then, that frequency is pushing it, but nobody is working on ferrites yet, that I've heard of.

"What we did was melt pure iron, then spray it through a nozzle in dry nitrogen. That broke it up into tiny droplets that cooled right away and fell into a pan. Then a little chemistry to put a thin oxide coating on each one, so the surface wouldn't be too conductive and cause a lot of eddy currents when they got together in a mass. I forget the details, but it's written down. After that we mixed it with a ceramic slurry to mostly keep the particles from touching each other, so we could shape it in a mold and fire it. Presto, powdered iron core! And she's right, the magnetic amplifier that does the modulation involves gapped cores. That took a little precision machining with a carbide wheel."

Robrecht opened a notebook and started writing. "So you think that's the answer, then? We should design the high-frequency magnetic parts with this powdered iron ceramic?"

"Sure. We have pretty good numbers on its performance, and we've made it before. We hung onto the stuff to make it, because we were afraid somebody else might want one of those crazy alternator transmitters. I hope you guys come up with some big power tubes before anybody takes it into their heads to do that again."

Robrecht leaned back and laughed. "Well, we've made some two-hundred-fifty-watt tubes, and Andy just built some kilowatt transmitters with five of them apiece. Will that do?"

"Maybe, until somebody wants ten kilowatts! Anyway, I'll dig out the data on the powdered iron material, and write it up for you. I ought to turn the whole thing over to AEW, they're the manufacturing people. Annie should be able to design your transformers right off the bat. Their plant can make them easy enough.

"So tell me about this flyback converter. Maybe I can work that thing out with straight calculations, and maybe not. Might have to build one that looks close, and then go to cut-and-try. Play with the windings, play with the gap. Might get there quicker if we start out a little bigger than we think we need."

"Cut-and-try? Like a ham project? I thought it should be possible to calculate it from the theory."

Bill shrugged. "Maybe, maybe not. I kind of know what a flyback circuit is, but I've never designed one. Neither have you. Or Andy. Let's see how close we get on the first try. You having fun with this project?"

"Yes, but every time I get back to the lab, Else looks straight at me and does everything but tap her foot. She wants me helping on the pentagrid tube. That's really the key to a modern receiver."

It was Bill's turn to laugh. "Modern? With tubes? How modern?"

"Pretty modern, as these things go. The latest thing in 1934."

* * *

John Grover was just outside the front door enjoying a cool breeze for a couple of minutes while he thought about the floor layout for the new production plant in Schwarza. Helga stuck her head out and called to him. "Martin Schreiber from the Department of Economic Resources is on the phone."

"Okay, I'll take it at my desk." He headed back inside.

A minute later he picked up. "Hello, Martin, what's happening?"

"We have an inquiry for something called a ventilator. From someone in Hamburg. Do you know what that is?"

"Well, I doubt you mean one for a mine, or you wouldn't be calling us. Yeah, I saw one in a TV show. It's a machine to breathe for a patient who can't. It's used sometimes for someone who's really sick, to keep them alive until they start to get better."

"I see. Is that something your people could make?"

"I doubt it. There's no tubes in the thing, it's all mechanical. Better try somebody else. The steamheads, maybe? Good luck."

John breathed a sigh of relief. The last thing GE needed was another distraction. Else Berding, still haunted by the carnage of Tilly's marauders tearing through her village, wasn't the only one getting twitchy about keeping GE's tube work on schedule. John himself had contributed ham gear to the new nation's defense, and it was getting used hard in the field.

* * *

The latest progress report from Kudzu Scientific Instruments showed about what John expected this early in the project. The strip chart recorder's sprocketed paper drive was working reasonably well, considering that it was nothing more than a geared-down model train motor running directly off the unregulated low voltage filament supply. Getting the chart speed more accurate and stable could wait; they could go into production with what they had, if they didn't have a decent speed regulator by the time everything else was working. And KSI had lined up a source for the chart paper rolls.

But the pen actuator was nowhere near strong enough to overcome the swerves and jerks when any small variation in the paper rolled past. And the ink feed to the end of the slender pointer arm vacillated between skipping altogether and spitting out droplets. Well, it was a modified switchboard meter movement from the AEW catalog. They needed something beefier, that could deliver enough mechanical force to trace out the signal coming from the EKG's amplifier without being bothered by drag. Clearly, it would have to be a brand-new design, done from a clean sheet of paper. Of course that meant more current, which would run down the battery faster, but that was hardly even a minor concern. If a patient was in any condition to be saved by an ambulance crew with an EKG and defibrillator, they would succeed in the first few minutes. Otherwise they wouldn't succeed at all.

John didn't need to bother Landon Reardon at AEW or his engineers about the pen actuator. They had the same report. For that matter, they could go visit KSI easily enough themselves to watch it in action. It was only a short walk across town.

And then there was the ink. What they'd tried was made for a fountain pen. It didn't seem to be suitable for a strip chart recorder. Maybe Lothlorien or Gribbleflotz could come up with something that would flow better. He picked up the phone to mention the thought to KSI. He was not about to call the chemistry gurus himself; a project manager didn't get between his suppliers and their suppliers. Not if he knew what was good for him.

And, of course, being based on a pivoted meter movement, the pen moved in an arc, not a straight line perpendicular to the paper advance. Naturally, the grid on the strip chart roll would have to be printed to match. John wasn't altogether happy about that. Neither were the medics who had to use it. But a straight-line pen actuator was not something anyone felt confident of getting to work reliably, if they wanted to hit their delivery date. And a day one way or another might mean a patient would survive who otherwise wouldn't. Nobody was forgetting that.

* * *

Andy Rogers worked out a circuit for an amplifier to pick up the signal from the left arm and right arm electrodes straddling the heart and boost it to a level that could drive the pen actuator. It used the new upgraded version of the same tube type as the oscillator stage of the ten-watt exciters they had just shipped to the navy. He put one together in quick-and-dirty breadboard form to test on the bench. Next, he wired up a simple attenuator circuit so he could run it with the old signal generator from his ham shack at home, and get a signal at the right level in the right frequency range to test the EKG amplifier. That didn't actually simulate the waveform of a real biological signal, it just replicated the relevant electrical properties.

The amplifier worked. It didn't oscillate, or produce the wrong gain or a lot of noise, or do anything else nasty. It moved the pen arm through the proper swing, as long as it wasn't getting dragged by the paper. The back end would probably need some changes when they got the real pen actuator, of course.

He brought it over to GE to try out on a live human. John put a couple of chair cushions on the conference room table, lay down, and unbuttoned his shirt. Gerry Hunsaker taped on a couple bits of copper foil in the proper places as electrodes. When Andy turned it on, the pen arm went flying back and forth from stop to stop, and everybody heard the familiar buzz of sixty-cycle electric power. He shut it down.

The room went silent.

Gerry Hunsaker looked at it, and said, "Got an idea."

He went out for the defibrillator from the ambulance, and connected just the EKG leads. Left arm, right arm, right leg. He turned it on and got a trace on screen. "You'll be glad to know your heart looks just fine to me, John. Of course, that's not a medical opinion. I'm not a doctor." Then he unclipped the right leg lead. The trace on-screen promptly went crazy. It was mostly off-screen.

Gerry clipped the lead back on. The trace settled down. He shut it off and straightened up. "We need to find out what that lead does."

Everybody looked at everybody else. It was becoming obvious what needed to be done, but nobody wanted to say it, not when an irreplaceable piece of up-time lifesaving gear was involved. It was time for the project manager to weigh in. "Gerry, will you let us look inside?"

Gerry looked down, sighed, and silently nodded.

The steadiest hands in the lab belonged to Heinz Bennemann, the general technician who had built most of Else's experimental tube models. He studied the unit's outside, then went for some tools. They'd decided to do the examination right there in the conference room, away from anyone who might wander by and cause a distraction or bump something. Isaack Liefrinck laid out a few sheets of paper where they could put down every screw and identify it with a number, while he sketched out where it went in a lab notebook.

Two minutes later the cover was off and Heinz had it resting upside-down on the table, so everyone could see where the connectors came in. Gerry cautioned, "Don't touch anything inside just because it's turned off. Remember what the manual said about dielectric soak-in. The big capacitor could still be hot."

Robrecht te Winkel picked up a magnifying glass and leaned in to see where the wire from the right leg terminal went. The magnifying glass had a plastic frame, not a metal one. He tilted it a little and moved it from side to side. The only place it seemed to go was a small metal box that covered part of a circuit board. There was a broad copper circuit trace running along the foot of the box all around its periphery, except for a narrow gap where a notch in the box let four fine circuit tracks enter.

Robrecht straightened up, staring at it. Then he looked up at the lights overhead, and his hands started to move. "I see it..." He paused, searching for words. "There is an electric field in the room. The lights are connected to the room wiring. It carries sixty-cycle AC at a hundred and twenty volts, yes? There are other things here connected to different voltages. Grounded plumbing in the sink? Other things? So, between any conductive objects at different voltages there is an electric field. And this"—he waved a hand at the device on the table—"is in the middle of it. If nothing is connected to it, it is at perhaps fifty volts or so relative to earth ground. And according to Maxwell's Equations, a space where there is a changing electric field is mathematically equivalent to a current flow. Not very much current here, the frequency is low and the charged bodies are small while the spacings are large, but 'not very much' is not the same as zero. In practice, all these bodies act together as a collection of capacitors, with tiny AC currents flowing through them. Enough to couple into the patient electrodes somehow and add a voltage to the measuring circuit. The effect is small, but so is the signal from the patient's heart. And then we amplify everything. Just how it couples in, I don't yet see. But enough to cause the large interference we saw.

"But this—" he pointed at the little box inside, with the magnifying glass still in his hand "—is a closed unipotential surface. It surrounds everything connected to the two leads that bring us the heart signal. The amplifier. Everything on that surface is at the same voltage. The voltage on the right leg. That is the average voltage on the patient's body, I suppose. Not the voltage on the lights overhead. Or the voltage at ground. Or some other voltage near the patient but not the same.

"So if the voltage on the box is the same as the average voltage of the two heart leads, then there is no electric field in the space between them. No current is driven into the electrodes. There must be more to it than that, I wonder what the impedance of the electrodes is? But this is what the right leg lead is for. It provides the voltage to this unipotential shell." He pointed to Andy's amplifier. "Now we have to figure out how to apply it to this. And still get the output to the pen. And get power into it without violating the leakage current specification. We must remember that."

As he was speaking, Helga Armbruster had been moving around the table with a camera, taking close-up pictures of what they could see inside, now that Grantville had film again. Finished, she returned to taking notes.

While Heinz put the covers back on, John just quietly looked on, taking in what he'd just seen and heard. Well, that was the difference between a ham and an electronics engineer. Hams understood circuit design well enough. They could do some very impressive things with just that knowledge and the reference books that went with it. But an engineer understood electromagnetic fields and advanced math at a much deeper level, with the ability to apply that theoretical knowledge to practical problems.

John and Conrad had understood that from the company's beginnings; it was why they had tried so hard to hire Else. But Robrecht's talent was of a different order. Else was smart, any college physics student had to be smart. She had been that kind of student, for all practical purposes, in Landon

Reardon's physics study group three years earlier. But Professor Liefrinck had been able to hand-pick Robrecht from among all the students he knew. It showed.

* * *

A lot of curious eyes were gathered around Andy and Robrecht as they made one more eyeball check of the test hookup to their flyback converter, and set one of Heinz's bench safety boxes over it. This contraption was nothing to take chances with.

A defibrillator worked by delivering a shock of two hundred or so watt-seconds of energy to the patient in twenty milliseconds, between a pair of electrodes placed to drive the current right through the heart. It did the job by shocking the misbehaving natural pacemaker to a frozen stop for a fraction of a second or thereabouts, so it could get its act back together and resume its proper pace. The arithmetic was simple. Two hundred watt-seconds delivered in twenty milliseconds is ten thousand watts. No battery a pair of big, strong men could carry around would be able to deliver that kind of power, but a big capacitor could. Up-time, it would have been an electrolytic capacitor, with a microscopically thin aluminum oxide dielectric formed by chemical action on the surface of a rolled-up foil electrode. Grantville had yet to master the design and manufacture of electrolytic capacitors. Some people were working on an alternative. Naturally, they expected it to come out bigger and heavier than an electrolytic with the same capacity. Maybe a lot bigger and heavier. They'd put wheels under the damn thing, if they had to. Today's capacitor bank had been scrounged from a home-brewed transmitter project that had never been completed.

The flyback converter's job was to cycle between taking microsecond bursts of power out of the battery at a current it could deliver, and passing them on to the capacitor. Charging the capacitor would take perhaps ten seconds or so, at an average rate of a little over a hundred watts, hopefully at about eighty percent efficiency. And then, look out.

It was inspired by a circuit in an old-time TV, that built up magnetic energy in the picture tube's horizontal deflection coils while it swept the spot horizontally across the screen painting the picture, and then abruptly dumped it into the high-voltage circuit that accelerated the beam toward the screen, all while the spot flew back to the left edge between scan lines. That was why it was called a flyback circuit.

The defibrillator's flyback converter didn't have a horizontal deflection coil, or a horizontal sync pulse from a TV station to trigger each cycle. So it needed the custom-made coupled inductor Robrecht and Bill had designed around a gapped powdered iron core, and it needed to be self-timing.

The inductor had something of an antique look. Its equivalent from the 1960s would have been wound with magnet wire insulated with a thin, smooth coating of pinhole-free polyimide or some similar synthetic polymer, compact and with good thermal conductivity from the interior to the outer surface for effective cooling. Grantville's chemical industry was years away from making anything like that. This was a coil Samuel Morse would have recognized. Like the helically wound cotton-thread covering prevalent from the 1840s to the early twentieth century, this one had two layers of fine linen yarn wound in opposite directions for improved reliability and insulation breakdown. Like most well-designed high-voltage windings of that era, this one had acid-free paper between the layers. The production version would be vacuum-impregnated with varnish for moisture resistance and additional breakdown voltage integrity.

Several of the lab's meters were coupled up to test points in the circuit, and the scope was connected across the resistor that monitored the current waveform flowing through the transmitter tube that switched the battery current on and off during each cycle. Hopefully, that would give them a picture of the circuit's operation as the inductor cycled, first taking in a pulse of energy from the battery and then dumping it into the capacitor through the output winding and rectifier tube.

Everybody looked at everybody else, nodded, and then Heinz closed the battery switch and kept his hand on it. It was his lab, after all.

The battery current ammeter pegged with an audible tink, and then smoke started pouring out of the open back side of the box. Heinz cut the switch fast. The view through the metal screen set into the front of the safety cover revealed red-hot wire, blackened magnet-wire insulation, a charred spot on the wooden table top directly underneath the coil, and a tiny flame still flickering on the primary winding. The tube was the only thing that looked okay, but then, it was oversized for the job. Else wasn't planning to get around to a mid-sized transmitter tube until they got the receiver tubes done.

Andy put it into words. "Geez, the tube must never have switched off when it hit the peak current setting."

That was obvious. Once the magnetic field in the core had passed the maximum the powdered iron could support, there was nothing to limit how high the current could go except the resistance of the wiring and that big tube's cathode emission—which was plenty. Their circuit design needed another look, for sure.

Up-time, they could have just bought a little integrated circuit that had all the control functions built in. For that matter, they could have bought a set of big, fat switching transistors and rectifier diodes instead of reaching for re-purposed transmitter tubes.

Robrecht was wondering just how many of the small low-power tubes they would need for the control functions to make the main tube cycle on and off the way it was supposed to. And not lock up in a funny state if it started up wrong. He mentally kicked himself for trying to make it work with as few components as possible; this beast had to be dependable. It was life-saving equipment.

As the smoke dissipated, possible schemes for the output circuit that shaped the actual shock were going through his head, even while he was still considering possible approaches to controlling the flyback cycle. Regardless, he wasn't in any doubt that he and Andy would get it done. After all, they wouldn't be the first to build a working electrocardiograph and defibrillator. Even with vacuum tubes.

Wild Flowers And Nailed Hearts

Natalie Silk

Zaborstadt

It was a perfectly sunny day for Dora and Anya to make their visits. Dora knocked on the rough-hewn door while her niece, Anya, stood three steps behind her. There was a click of the latch. Mira pushed a wayward, gray-streaked curl back into her cap before opening the door.

"Welcome! Come in!" Mira seemed very tired, but she still smiled warmly at her visitors.

Anya entered and waited for her eyes to adjust and immediately looked for Mother Tanya, who was sleeping soundly. Good. There would be no chance of receiving a nasty, bruise-worthy pinch if she got too close to the elderly woman. She touched her right arm where she had been delivered a hard-learned lesson during her first visit.

"Tell me, Dora, how is it with your niece's learning? Is she understanding making salves and medicine and midwifery?"

"Yes, she's learning very well." Dora turned to her niece with an appreciative smile, "Isn't this so?"

"Yes, I hope in Grantville I finish learning." Anya was still learning German. This wasn't easy as they primarily spoke Spanish at home.

"Grantville?" Mira seemed a little surprised.

"As a nurse."

"I see," was the only response.

Dora gave Anya a very subtle shake of her head.

Luckily Mira didn't notice. "I thought your aunt and uncle would rather you not go to Grantville. After all, I hear it's not a place for a young unmarried woman." Mira quickly amended her response when she saw Anya's crestfallen expression. "Perhaps you may go visit after you're married."

Anya had heard often enough the dangers and vices of the town, but now, though she understood, she also heard about all the wonders. Surely, that was reason enough to study in Grantville. Tia Dora and Tio Danel would never allow her to go to Grantville. Holding back tears, she made a quick and shallow curtsy and left. She wouldn't cry. Not now in front of everyone. She would wait until she was by herself in her hiding place in the woods. Away from her tia and tio's betrayal. She ran. Maybe she would run to Grantville instead. She dropped down on her knees under the familiar pine tree and, in spite of the pricks to her fingers and palms, she threw handfuls of brown pine needles while crying in frustration and humiliation. Throwing needles wasn't good enough. She stood up and slapped the rough trunk until her palms were raw and painful. She sat down hard. How would she ever get to Grantville? Boys could be apprenticed and even go to Grantville. *Why was life so unfair?* This thought made her cry even harder. She stomped her feet and pounded the ground. She didn't know how long she was there, but she realized that her crying was now a sniffle. She allowed herself one last good snuffle and wiped her eyes with the back of her scratched, dirty hands. She got up and brushed off the new skirt she and Tia had sewn from the coarse blue cloth they bought at the mercantile in town. Then forgetting herself, she ran her nose along her sleeve. She didn't want to go home. Not really. She wanted to be in Grantville. She reconciled herself that her fondest wish was useless and headed home.

She found Deborah playing in the front yard with a doll made from scraps. Roza and Simon would be home soon from their schools. As soon as Anya opened the door, Tio and Tia stopped talking.

"Anya." They both looked uncomfortable. Tia assessed her niece's wounded hands.

"What happened?"

She didn't answer. What could she say after such a betrayal?

Tia nudged Tio Danel's arm and nodded her head towards Anya. He stood up and faced her, clearing his throat and smoothing down his beard, before speaking. It was obvious to Anya that he was avoiding speaking to her. "Your tia and I apologize for causing you to be overwrought." Tia Dora nodded, and smiled to reassure her it was the truth.

Anya's silence worried Tia Dora. "Anya?"

She remembered that she was once a cared-for daughter of a man of means and a loving mother. She finally spoke. "You never intended for me to go to Grantville and become a true nurse. Why? Is it because of the cost of my attendance? Or because of the loss of my help about the house?" Part of her couldn't believe that she had found her bravery. "You'd rather have me tend to your home and your children."

"Grantville is not a place for a respectable young woman such as yourself."

Her father once told her that up-time women exposed their legs by wearing trousers and therefore had questionable morals. However, up-time women went to university. It was reasonable to infer that Grantville wasn't all that bad. "And yet, it holds places of great education and mechanical marvels."

"We want you to be married with your own family. To be happy and safe," Tia said.

Anya was about to reply but fell silent when she heard the latch rattle and the door creak open behind her. Deborah stopped short, hugging her doll a little closer when the three looked at her.

"Put your doll away and go fetch water," her mother said.

By her curious expression, the little girl knew there was something being discussed and she wanted to know.

"Come along!" Deborah jumped from being startled and moved quickly. She put her doll down on her mother's stool by the hearth and left with the bucket.

No one spoke until the latch clicked in place. "We won't speak of this again. I will find a respectable young man for you from a good family," Tio said.

Dora added, "And you'll continue to learn the midwifery arts from Rhea and how to prepare medicines from me."

Danel slapped the table for finality. "It's decided." He got up, straightened his coat, and announced, "I'll be out in the barn."

Dora scoffed. "What shall you do out there? Didn't you tend to the horses already?"

"I want to be with my own thoughts, wife."

The right side of Dora's mouth pulled up, and she looked up as if pleading to the heavens. She looked at Anya and then stood to go to the shelf for a bowl. She returned to the table and reached over to the water jug. She placed the water-filled bowl on the table and went to get freshly laundered bandages, soap, and a jar of salve. "Let me tend to your hands.

When I'm done, I want you to help me with supper," adding more gently, "If you're able."

With her hands clean and bandaged, she resigned herself to readying their meal.

Deborah came inside leaving a trail of sloshed water from a too-full bucket. Dora was not too surprised.

"Anya, would you help me?"

Anya set aside the shovel she was using to cover a pot with hot embers. Of course she would help her cousin, it was expected of her. The sarcastic thought didn't burn her already hurt heart. She wrapped her bandaged hand around the bucket's rope handle and lifted it. It was truly too heavy for her little cousin—even if she used both hands. She thought again how unfair things were: Simon would soon be apprenticed and have the opportunity to see Grantville for himself.

Danel slowly walked from the barn with his head down and hands clasped behind his back, contemplating the idea; how to find a suitable husband for his niece and ask his brother for the dowry. Finding a match would be easy enough: he would speak with the rabbi who would suggest that he consult with Zaborstadt's shadchan, a matchmaker. He hoped the rabbi would help with finding a suitable match, saving Danel the cost of a matchmaker. He returned to the house satisfied.

"Anya, Dora. I will speak with the rabbi."

"Your tio *and I* will speak with the rabbi," Dora corrected.

"No. I will do this, wife. And I will write to your papa for a dowry."

Just by his wife's narrowed eyes and the way she set her mouth that made her lips look as if they disappeared, he knew he was in trouble. Corresponding with his brother was not her concern. And even if Yeshua didn't provide a dowry, it might be of no consequence. This was not Spain.

"Now I must attend to my evening prayers."

"Leave us," she said to Anya and Deborah. "Go call Simon and Roza. They should be home by now."

When they were alone, Dora did her best to talk over her husband's prayers. "We should speak with the rabbi together."

Danel prayed louder and turned his back to his wife, giving the appearance that he didn't hear her. "I specifically said that we should wait in asking for Anya's dowry."

He continued to ignore her.

She put her hands on her hips. "Hmmph," she said, and went back to ladling the stew into bowls. It was no accident that Danel's serving was a little less than expected that evening. He didn't say much during the meal other than the occasional acknowledgement when Simon, Deborah, and Roza chattered about their day.

* * *

Supper was long finished and the fire was banked with Anya attending it for the night while the rest of the household was in bed.

Danel and Dora spoke softly; neither could sleep. "I reconsidered, Husband. Speak with the rabbi." Dora paused. "I will miss having her about the house. But I've got on well enough before and I'm sure I can make do without her."

"Hmm. Her German could be much improved."

Dora chuckled quietly. "Do you recall the Fugger's representative? Gephardt."

"Gebhardt. Yes, Horst Gebhardt. I recall him well. By his attentions to our niece, I'm sure he wanted to secure more than orange juice for his master. It was fortunate that she knew even less German then. You want to betroth our niece to a man who will care little for her wellbeing? And who belonged to the Church?"

"Of course not! On both accounts. But he was a young man of means."

"Her lack of the language may be an advantage. After all, she's so willful and spirited. And stubborn." He was about to add that Dora was very much the same, but the thought of having to spend a night in the barn kept him silent. He spent far too many nights there. Instead, "I'll speak to the rabbi on this matter soon enough." He waited for her response.

"Tomorrow. I also think discussing such matters with his wife is a better choice. I should speak to her." She had an idea. "Ask them both to come here before Shabbot."

Couldn't his wife settle on one idea? "I'll speak to him privately first."

"Wha—"

"*I* will speak with him privately *first*, wife." He rolled on to his side away from Dora. "Sleep well." He smiled when he felt his wife settle with a "humph." It was such a rarity when he had the final word.

* * *

While riding his horse to the rabbi's home, Danel pondered how he would approach the subject. Today would be the first opportunity and he hoped to leave a good impression. He saw a coat carefully draped over a branch of a tree, then saw a man sitting by the Saale River. He had almost passed the scene before he realized it was the rabbi fishing. Danel reined in his horse sharply and turned around.

"Rabbi Samuel?"

The rabbi looked over. "Ah, Herr Nahon! Good day!"

"I didn't expect to see you here." Why would he say such a foolish thing? He jumped off and led his horse over to the rabbi. The grass and water would do the animal good.

The rabbi smiled. "I allow my more advanced students to teach the younger boys on occasion. Since I have no need to counsel today, I shouldn't let a wonderful opportunity such as this," nodding towards his fishing rod, "to pass."

"Of course, Rabbi." Danel looked at the water then back at him. "My wife, Dora and I were wondering—"

"How is your wife?"

"She's well. Thank you for asking. My wife and I were wondering. We have concerns for our niece, Anya. Would you and Rabbanit Esther care to pay us a visit?" Why did he stumble over his thoughts? He always found the right words when he was in the shop conducting business or directing his employees. Why now?

"What is the matter with your niece? Is she ill again?"

"No, no. She's well. I have come to a decision that she should be wedded."

"Ah, I see."

"I would ask that you and your wife come join us for a meal. After Shabbot."

"Most gracious of you. Yes, I shall tell my wife that we will come after celebrating the Shabbot."

Then Danel recalled that Dora told him to invite the rabbi and his wife *before* the Shabbot. No matter, the invitation was made.

"Do you fish?"

"No, Rabbi. I don't."

The rabbi nodded. "This is an up-time-style fishing rod. It was a gift from some of my students. Quite unexpected, but very much cherished just the same." There was a sudden tugging towards the water and he got very excited, "Look! Look! Another fish. I have caught another one!" He turned the little handle on the reel. He pulled back and out flew his catch. Danel watched as the rabbi quickly took the hook out of the struggling fish and dropped it in a basket with a lid along with two other equally unfortunate (and now dead) friends. "A fine meal for my family."

"Yes. It will make a fine meal."

The rabbi assessed Danel and then offered the pole to him. "You shall try. It's very simple. Just a quick back and forth and then a flick. Just like this," he said while demonstrating the movements. "Out there," pointing to a distance in the water.

Danel turned with his back to his companion and imitated the demonstrated motion then flicked. He jumped in surprise at a howl from behind and turned. The hook caught on the rabbi's shirt. Actually, it not only caught the poor man's shirt, apparently it also caught his chest. The rabbi yelped and paddled his hands in front of him as if swatting invisible insects. Danel, in his horror, tugged the fishing line without thinking. This caused the rabbi to howl louder. Somehow, the rabbi disengaged the hook from his body.

Mortified with embarrassment, "Rabbi, please accept my sincerest apologies! I didn't mean to cause such harm."

"Herr Nahon, I believe I must return home now. Please expect my wife and myself after the last Shabbot prayers."

"Of course, Rabbi. I'm so very sorry, Rabbi."

* * *

A while after the evening meal was finished, Dora asked, "You've been very quiet since you came home. Why is this? I would think that you would be in a better mood since the rabbi agreed to come."

"Yes, the rabbanit and he will come. After the last Shabbot prayers."

"The last—!? Didn't I specifically say *before* Shabbot?!"

"Yes, yes. You did. I've decided it would be better for them to be here afterwards."

"Of course, you did." She gave him the same disgusted expression that was so very familiar to him and then softened slightly. "You haven't truly answered my question: why so quiet?"

He told her about the fishing incident. She sat down—hard—on her stool by the hearth. If it were any other man who had the misfortune of a hook in his chest and any other man who put it there, she would laugh after her initial horror. She looked up as if she were addressing the heavens, "Why me?! Why us? Why must we be punished so?!"

* * *

Dora sat next to her gentle friend Tovah behind the curtain with the other women during Shabbot services. Danel begged her to tend to the home; but she thought that Anya and Roza could manage the remaining tasks and mind Deborah. The meal being served would be light. Still, listening to all the whisperings, she regretted her decision to attend.

Dora did her best to ignore what she heard, but it made her so angry. *"His good wife spent so much time tending to her poor husband's wounds and mending his shirt." "It was fortunate no infection set in." "Isn't it odd the Nahons are the cause of so many strange events?" "It is. I wonder if they are being punished for some misdeed." "You do know they had to leave their home. I heard it was because of some disgrace." "Tsk-tsk-tsk." "And the Rabbi and his wife will* still *visit later today." "Truly, he is a good man for doing so." "Yes, we are most fortunate to have such a man as our beloved Rabbi."*

Dora looked at her friend, who looked at her at the same time. The woman smiled and patted her hand. The reassurance was welcome but did little to soothe her. Dora smiled back, feigning that she was not in the least embarrassed at the gossip and criticism around her. A few of these women shouldn't judge too harshly (if what she heard during her visits to market had any truth to it).

* * *

After the meal was finished and Anya and their children were told to leave, Rabbanit Esther and Dora sat side-by-side near the hearth quietly watching and listening to their husbands still sitting at the table discussing the matter at hand. Rabbi Samuel smacked his lips, smoothed his beard, and put his mug down. "This is very good."

Danel took up the pitcher and poured the rabbi some more orange juice. "I'm glad you enjoy it."

"Dora," said the rabbanit, "How is Anya? I see her hands are bandaged."

Danel saw his wife's discomfort.

"Only a little mishap. I assure you," was her only reply.

The rabbi intervened. "It was fortunate that it was no great injury, and I'm sure with your ministrations, Anya will heal quickly. Which brings me to the matter at hand. My wife and I are here to discuss your niece."

"Yes," Danel saw his wife looking at him encouragingly. He could tell that she truly wanted to take up the conversation, but knew it would not be permitted. "It's time that Anya becomes a proper wife and—hopefully—a mother."

"Husband," Esther said, "My sister, Noemi, has a good son." Then to Dora, "The youngest of their four children, the only one not married. Noemi married well, I must say."

"Of course, of course." Danel chuckled. "Efraim. He's a fine young man. Industrious, clever, and learned."

"Husband," Dora asked, "How does he earn a living?"

"We would desire our niece to live comfortably," Danel said.

The rabbi nodded, smiled, and sat back in his chair. "He has completed his apprenticeship as a clockmaker and now is employed as an assistant in the shop. He even studied the mechanics of up-time clocks."

"Husband, please ask the rabbi how old is Efraim."

"Our niece is very young and delicate." He impressed himself how he managed to keep a steady expression while he recalled Anya defending herself from a local ruffian who wanted to "admire" her skirts.

"Hmm. Efraim is now in his nineteenth year."

Dora stood and walked over to the door. When she opened it, Anya almost tumbled in along with Roza. "You both may as well come in. You'll hear better." They looked ashamed, but they came inside anyway and sat by the two women at the hearth.

Rabbi Samuel continued, "We'll arrange for you to visit my brother-in-law Isaiah and his family to meet their youngest. Hopefully, you'll see that Efraim," he said looking at Anya, "is indeed a fine young man for your niece."

"Where do they live?"

"They call it the outskirts of Grantville, but it's Grantville nonetheless."

From the corner of Danel's eye, he saw his niece immediately look even more interested. He turned his head so that she would see his expression that told her to contain herself. This was a delicate matter at hand and he wanted it to go well.

He faced the rabbi and cleared his throat. "Anya desires to go to Grantville."

"Yes. We understand that she wants to learn nursing skills. This is a concern of ours—and will be of my sister-in-law as well when we discuss this matter—it's more important that she becomes a proper wife and mother to Efraim and his children."

"My husband,"—Esther looked at the rabbi—"and also keep a proper home."

Danel looked at the two women and quickly looked away. Dora's expression told him he shouldn't have even mentioned Anya wanting to become a nurse. "Anya is now satisfied with learning the midwifery skills." Then he added with a nod to his niece, "and to be a proper and good wife. We are agreed." Danel stood. "We shall meet and discuss matters with Efraim's father."

Dora and Esther stood when their husbands got up from their seats. Dora went to a large crockery and withdrew a small burlap bag. "We want to give this to you." She handed it to Esther. "Oranges."

"Thank you. Very kind."

* * *

Everyone stood outside in the yard as Rabbi Samuel and Rabbanit Esther took their leave. Anya waited for them to be well down the road. "Tia, do you think my husband will allow me to become a nurse? Will we live in Grantville?" For the first time in what seemed to be a long time, she was hopeful that she would finally get her wish.

Tia Dora turned to her and smiled. "I'm glad that you're enthusiastic about marrying. Perhaps you should wait until your tio meets this young man and sees for himself if he will be a good man for you. Then we must write to your father and see what kind of dowry he will provide for you. Without one, you may not be able to marry at all."

"Dora," Danel interrupted, "our people in Germany are not like our people in Spain."

Dora scuffed. "Such ridiculous thoughts. Our people are the same when it comes to their children."

* * *

Rabbi Samuel sat beside Danel in the wagon on the way to Grantville. It was barely sunrise. Reaching Efraim's family's home would take several hours. Danel thought about his own courtship. He hoped (and prayed) that his people in Germany were very different. If not, then the courtship would take the better part of a year, and discussions of a dowry would take a small part of that time. The morning meal churned in his stomach. What if his brother refused to provide for his daughter? Would Efraim's father allow his son to marry a poor, dowry-less girl? He turned his body enough to look at the small crate of oranges behind them.

"What is the matter?"

"It's nothing, Rabbi."

"Hmm," the rabbi nodded.

They rode on in silence until the rabbi pointed to another road that led them to a part of Grantville that was familiar to Danel—he made deliveries there on occasion. Yet, he was unfamiliar with this family. He was rather embarrassed: he really thought he knew Grantville's families very well. He looked forward to adding this home to his route.

"Ah, there's Isaiah, Noemi, and Efraim."

Danel reined in the horses as Isaiah and his wife stepped forward. The couple wore clothes made of green and black cloth although the colors were slightly faded.

"Welcome to our home, Herr Nahon," said Isaiah. "Samuel, let me help you down."

"Thank you, Isaiah. Noemi, you look well."

"Thank you. How is Esther?"

"She's well and sends her good wishes."

Isaiah looked behind him at the young man who was wearing a white shirt and vest that looked new and then faced his guests. "This is our son, Efraim."

Efraim stepped forward and bowed. Danel returned the greeting. He tried not to cock an eyebrow when he realized their son was much the taller and he would need to crane his neck just to meet the boy's eyes when he talked to him.

Danel reached over the side of the wagon and lifted the crate of oranges. "Herr, please accept this. A few oranges for you and your family."

Isaiah's smile was warm in gratitude. "Thank you," he said as he took the crate.

Noemi picked up an orange, gave it two appreciative sniffs and placed it back with the others. She said to her husband, "It's a very generous gift."

"There's also a flask of juice that my wife made this morning. She hopes that you and your family enjoy it."

Isaiah nodded. "We will. Come, let us go inside. My wife has prepared a light meal and she'll pour each of us the juice instead of ale. You'll be introduced to my fine son and—"

Rabbi Samuel interrupted. "Isaiah, you still allow your wife to pour ale?"

"There is no harm in it and she doesn't drink such things."

"Hmm. We shall discuss this matter at another time."

Danel wondered why Noemi couldn't pour ale and reminded himself to ask on their way home.

Danel looked around. It was a spacious house, showing the family's wealth. Although the furnishings were sparse, it was still comfortable. *"Of course," Danel thought, "Efraim is the youngest of their children. He must be the one to take care of his parents in their age. Yet, wouldn't one of the older daughters, even if married, want to remain home to take care of them instead?"* He was grateful that he was ushered to their table: he could speak comfortably with Efraim without hurting his neck.

"Tell me, Efraim, how is your work?"

He looked at his parents for their cue of a nod; receiving one, he cleared his throat and began. "It's very good. I enjoy repairing up-time clocks."

"Truly? I have never seen one closely. Even in my travels to Grantville."

"May I show you one?"

This visit was turning out very well. Not only was he impressed with Efraim, but Efraim was also able to satisfy his curiosity. Fascinating machines, these up-time marvels. The wonder of it.

"Please excuse me. I'll be only a moment."

"Of course! Of course!" Danel waited for Efraim to leave. "Your son is a fine young man, indeed. Just speaking with him momentarily told me his measure."

Isaiah and Noemi beamed. Even Rabbi Samuel smiled with pride.

"Thank you, Herr Nahon. We strove to raise our sons to be industrious," said Isaiah.

"I shall add that he is well educated," said the rabbi. "I personally saw to this task myself as his uncle."

Danel was about to add a comment, just as he heard Efraim enter the room. "This is what I was speaking of, Herr Nahon." He offered the small clock to Danel.

It felt odd to the touch: it looked like well-polished wood, but it wasn't. He ran a fingernail along one line of the dark brown "grain." Then he turned it over and saw two empty cylinder-shaped grooves.

"The up-timers put a thing called a—" Efraim searched for the word. "'*Batting-re*.' Yes, that's the correct word. They use a '*batting-re*' to make the clock work. Nothing else for this clock."

This piqued Danel's curiosity even more. "Do you have such a thing to show me?"

"Unfortunately no, Herr Nahon."

"Then how shall you make it work?"

"It is something that I'm pondering. Perhaps I can use the parts from another clock. I don't know yet."

Danel handed back the clock. Efraim excused himself, left the room, and returned quickly.

"Yes, a very fine young man."

* * *

The meal ended and it seemed that everyone was relaxed in each other's company. Danel spoke directly to Isaiah, "If this is agreeable to you, I would like Efraim to call on Anya in the future."

"Yes, yes. Of course." Isaiah turned to his wife. "Don't you agree?"

"Yes, Husband. I do." She smiled.

Danel had another idea, "Efraim, come for dinner Monday next and meet my niece. You will see how fine a cook she is. Of course, Isaiah, I extend this invitation to you and your wife as well."

They exchanged a look and Danel wondered why they didn't agree to this. "Thank you, Herr Nahon. But we shall decline your very generous offer. Perhaps, my wife's brother-in-law and sister will attend in our stead." Then he quickly added, "My wife and I would truly enjoy the invitation, it's simply that my business, you see, takes me away from so many engagements."

Danel nodded. "Of course, I understand." Yet, he felt there was something that Isaiah was hiding from him. The fault wasn't with the Nahons. If that were true, then why have Efraim meet his niece?

* * *

Anya's rolling and circling thoughts gained momentum each day closer to Efraim's arrival. Her daily chores, assisting Rhea, and learning from Tia Dora hardly stopped her mind from worrying about the visit. Even taking the time to wash her good dress and cap didn't relieve her fretting. Actually, the activity compounded the matter. She even washed her hair. Of course, Tia Dora reminded her several times that she should keep her head covered during the visit.

"I don't want you pulling off your cap like the time when Frau Stein and Tovah came to purchase oranges. How horrified! How embarrassing! You must be modest and present yourself as a proper young woman. Do you understand?"

"I won't embarrass you, Tia. I promise."

"Good."

But tia brought up the incident several more times before Efraim's visit, which was maddening to Anya.

* * *

Anya was deep in worrying thoughts while on her way to market the day before Efraim's visit. Only a few paces away from the market square she saw a ruffian and his friends attempting to "*admire*" a young woman's skirts with a long branch. The poor girl, seeming to be both appalled and embarrassed, squeaked and quickly scuttled away while smoothing her skirts back in place. Anya remembered the lead ruffian very well: it was shortly after she had shorn her hair.

Anya inhaled deeply, refusing to slow her pace. She was not going to let anyone force her to change her path. She looked at that same boy narrow-eyed as she walked past them. There was no mistaking that her expression said: "*I dare you.*" He remembered her and took a step back. He also stopped his friends to let Anya pass. She continued to scowl at them. She looked forward again when the group was a few paces behind her. Her disgusted, defiant expression smoothed to a satisfied smile. No one would ever get the better of her. She felt triumphant. She continued on her way to buy, with funds the household could barely afford, the spices she needed to prepare the lamb.

* * *

Anya overheard Tio Danel whisper to her tia, "I recognize one of the horses. Its owner is one of the men at the synagogue. I wonder if the other horse and cart belongs to Efraim."

Tia whispered through a smile, "Never mind, just greet our guests."

Tio Danel walked up when the two-horse cart came to a stop in front of their home. "Welcome, Rabbi! Welcome, Rabbanit!" he said bowing to each. He helped Esther down. "Ah, Efraim! Welcome, young man!" He bowed. The nervous and almost timid man unfolded his legs from the back of the cart and caught himself from stumbling when he got down. It took him a moment to bow.

Anya did her best not to smile. Even when he bowed, he still towered over Tio Danel. Although he was fine-looking, his face was too thin.

She watched her uncle putting Efraim at ease by leading the young man by the arm. "Come, I'll introduce you to my family. My wife, Dora." She saw Efraim look around as if he needed to alleviate some discomfort; but his eyes always came back to her, which in turn made her feel nervous.

Dora curtsied. "Welcome, Rabbi and Esther. And welcome, Efraim."

"My children, Simon, Roza, and Deborah." Each child bowed or curtsied as they were introduced. "And this is my niece, Anya." She didn't want to make eye contact with him. Casting her eyes down, she gave a timid, quick bob of a curtsy. Her eyes quickly darted to her tia and then back to the ground. She couldn't tell whether Tia Dora approved or disapproved.

"Danel, show the Rabbi and the Rabbanit inside. I'll remain here with Efraim and Anya," and to her son and daughters, "Go play, children." She had barely finished before they scurried off.

"Of course, wife." Danel answered while ushering the Rabbi and his wife inside their home. "There's fine orange juice for you both."

Dora sat down on her stool which she had placed by the door earlier just for this purpose. "Efraim, how goes your work?"

He nervously cleared his throat, "Very well."

"I hear that you make and repair clocks. Even up-time clocks. Do tell."

"Yes, it's most fascinating to me. I hope someday to have my own shop. Perhaps also in Grantville."

Grantville. Anya's heart skipped at the mention of the most wonderful place in the world (aside from her home in Spain). "Nursing to be," Anya blurted out.

"I beg your pardon?"

"Please excuse my niece. She is still learning German." Dora followed with, "and the midwife arts." Anya knew that expression, thin lipped, narrow eyes: the *"You disappoint me, but I'm not going to scold or punish you. For now."* look.

"Yes, yes. As my uncle and aunt told me." Anya could tell he wanted to say something else when he looked at her. She cast her eyes down again. If only she knew better German. Hopefully she would learn to love this man, live in Grantville, and be permitted to become a nurse. She hoped he would allow such a dream.

Dora stood up. "Come, let's go inside. Anya, you'll help me serve." She looked around and saw Simon, Roza, and Deborah nearby. In short, clipped words, "Children! Come inside!" Dora went into the house with Anya and Efraim following.

"A most wonderful drink! Orange juice," They heard Esther say as she entered.

"I'm glad. We don't drink it often. We allow our customers and guests to enjoy it."

Roza and Deborah scooted past Efraim, almost bumping into his back. He turned around, startled.

"Where's your brother?"

"He's coming." Roza answered before her sister did. Deborah frowned; she looked as if she wanted to answer.

"Hmm. Roza, help Anya." Then she remembered the custom and prayer. "After you wash your hands, then help Deborah wash her hands."

"Mama, I can do it," Deborah said.

"Of course. But your sister will help you. Sit down at your place when you finish." Then Dora said to Efraim, "Please sit here," indicating an empty place with an open hand. "You'll be next to Anya when she's done helping me." Then she quickly added, "After you wash your hands, of course."

He went to the wash basin while the two little girls watched him pouring water over his hands and saying the prayer.

Anya's cousin finally came in, shutting the door with a slam that startled his mother.

"Wash your hands, Simon." He looked around at the guests and then at his sisters and Efraim, who was saying each word slowly so the girls could repeat after him while they poured water over their hands. Deborah interrupted Efraim, insisting that she could hold the pitcher by herself. Simon was about to say something at this change of routine and thought better of it. In all Anya's worrying ever since Tio announced that she was to be married to Efraim, she now noticed that Simon seemed to be brooding over something. She would need to ask him later.

Tia Dora began ladling food into serving platters and bowls that she had brought with her to her marriage. Anya thought her tia was careful in setting each serving bowl and platter down. Unfortunately, one of them was chipped. Tia looked at her, momentarily embarrassed.

"I'll serve this dish," Tia said looking down at the chipped bowl.

Once everyone was at the table, Tia Dora and she began serving. Tia Dora carefully held the chipped bowl, covering the defect with her left hand. Anya's lamb and gravy dish would be the last. She followed tia around the table, serving each helping.

"I must tell you, Efraim, Anya prepared this especially for today's occasion. It's her best dish. Of course, she's an excellent cook." Dora beamed at her niece and Anya returned the affection with a bashful smile and down-cast eyes.

"I'm sure I will like it," he said, turning to Anya with a slight smile.

Deborah looked down at her plate, "Mama, I thought we were going to eat the fish that Simon and Papa caught today."

They all looked at one another.

Anya saw the rabbi exchange glances with his wife. She then saw her tio and tia's uneasiness and how they were doing their best to hide their embarrassment.

"Mama is preparing the fish for the winter," Tio offered.

"Yes, for another day," the rabbi replied.

"Rabbi, please. Will you give us the prayer?" The rabbi looked at Danel and then at the variety of food on the table. "Of course." The rabbi said the prayer for the bread which was the blessing for the entire meal. Anya waited to take her place at the table until the rabbi finished. The men and Simon threw their napkins over their left shoulders. In spite of her nervous stomach, she realized how hungry she was and began to eat in earnest.

"Don't you agree, niece of mine?"

She swallowed and looked at Tio Danel. "What?" Everyone was looking at her, waiting for an answer. She hadn't even noticed the conversation.

She saw that Efraim took advantage of the distraction by giving a single *cough* and tucking another piece of sliced bread into his napkin.

"We were wondering how much you enjoy learning midwifery from Rhea and helping Frau Nahon with the infirm."

This was already asked, but Anya thought they were making casual conversation. She did her best to hide her uneasiness. "Oh, it is well. I like it fine."

"You've finished your lamb, Ephraim," said Dora. "Would you like more?"

"Yes, thank you." He quickly added, "It is very good."

Dora barely waited for his reply, plopping another serving on his plate with a smile. "Anya's best dish."

Danel, Dora, Anya, and the children waved their guests off at the end of the visit.

"Anya, children, please go back inside."

Anya followed her cousins into the house but she slipped back out and hid behind the huge tree in the yard to eavesdrop.

She heard her aunt say, "You'll need to write to her father and tell him that Efraim has asked to marry his daughter."

"Of course, wife, of course."

"She'll need a dowry. Do demand that he provide one. A good one that is sizable."

"Demand? I shall ask him. And if he doesn't agree to provide the funds?"

She inhaled. "Can we, then?"

Anya didn't hear anything for a while, and then, "I don't want to ask Javier for a loan. We have two daughters to think of." She heard footsteps and peeked long enough to see that her tio and tia were walking away from the house. She went inside and saw her cousin at the door.

"What is it, Simon?"

He looked down at his feet and shrugged.

"Tell me," she added more gently, "Please."

Still looking down, "You'll go live in Grantville."

"Yes, I'll need to live with my husband."

"You won't be living here."

Then she realized why he was so upset with her. Why he hadn't talked to her ever since the announcement that she was betrothed to Efraim. "Simon, I'm still here. And soon you will be apprenticed. I'll ask your papa to secure an apprenticeship for you in Grantville. You can live with us."

He looked at her, hopeful. "You'll do that?"

"Of course."

Satisfied, he smiled and went outside.

* * *

The shadows were lengthening when the cart left the Nahon household. It would be dusk just as they would arrive home. Efraim resumed his cramped place with his knees almost to his chest and his back to his uncle and aunt.

"Well, Efraim," his uncle said. "Anya seems to be a fine young woman. I hope her father will agree to give her hand to you."

"Yes, as do I," said his aunt. "Your mother tells me in confidence that your father will need to discuss with Danel a very delicate matter." She paused, shamed by the truth. "He has fallen on difficult times and currently doesn't have as much wealth as believed."

Efraim knew how difficult things were. The true reason for his parents not attending the day's visit was his father's meeting with an associate that might allow him to keep the business. He knew his father would allow him to marry Anya. Anya's dowry was desperately needed. "She seems very headstrong."

"It must be in the blood of the Spaniards," his uncle said. "Especially the women." Then added, "She doesn't know German very well so that may be to your advantage. But there is plenty of time. Danel will send a letter to his brother. I hope the reply will be favorable."

"Yes, a favorable one," his wife agreed.

Efraim was forced to eat the second helping of meat under Frau Nahon's watchful eyes, but he managed to sneak the first helping into his handkerchief. He ate the saved meat along with the bread until it was gone. He couldn't help himself; he was always hungry. He looked down at his now empty handkerchief. At least Anya could cook.

* * *

The muscular young man easily jumped down from the back of the wagon, which caused it to creak, relieved of a body that spent long hours hammering and bending metal. One of the two horses huffed and stomped as if understanding there would be relief from the wagon's load. "I thank you for allowing me to ride." He grabbed his sack.

The driver twisted slightly in his seat to look squarely at the young man. Just by the effort of the maneuver, it was obvious the years of hard labor had taken their toll on him. "You're welcome. I know your brother and his wife. You'll wish them well for me?"

"Yes, of course." He waved the kind stranger off and began walking down the road that would lead to Zaborstadt. After spending most of his travels avoiding highwaymen and common thieves and sleeping hidden in woods with only a blanket to keep him warm—the smoke of a fire would reveal him—he was grateful that someone had taken him this far.

He passed a farm on his right and a small home on his left. A little girl was playing out front. He stopped. A young woman came from around the back of the house carrying firewood. She was the most beautiful girl he had ever seen. He realized that he was staring when she frowned at him as she went into the house. He felt his cheeks flush. Embarrassed, he looked down at his feet and continued his journey.

He soon entered the town proper. "Excuse me, Herr. Where can I find the blacksmith?"

The man in an overly mended overcoat stopped and turned to assess this stranger, wondering whether he meant any harm. Deciding otherwise, the man pointed to his right and said, "Just a few paces that way."

The young man nodded his gratitude. "Thank you."

It seemed longer than a few paces, but he found his way. He was elated when he saw the smithy belonging to Benjamin. "Brother!"

Benjamin was in mid-strike on a red-hot horseshoe when he looked up. A huge smile transformed his sweating face. "Jakob! Wait! Let me finish." Three more clangs of his hammer and he allowed the water in a barrel to cool the metal. He put down his tools and the shoe on the anvil so that he could draw his little brother into a rib-crushing, affectionate hug. "Safe journey? Yes?"

Jakob gasped, "Yes...safe. You can put me down."

Benjamin released him. "Tovah will be glad to see you too. Let me finish my day's work, then we can go into the house. Even if it's not every day that we have visitors or even family, my customers demand their repairs and such done. You will tell me all the news of home while I work." He examined another horseshoe and placed it in the fire.

Jakob chuckled. "I see that you still work very hard. That has not changed." He casually dropped his sack and rolled blanket by a bench and began using the bellows to stoke the fire.

"How is Tovah?"

"All is fine with her. She keeps me well fed." Benjamin's brow creased. "How are Papa and Mama?"

"They are well. They miss you and Tovah."

"Ah, this is good. I mean that they are well—not that they miss us. What of Berta and her husband?"

Jakob paused and looked at the hot coals. "We're uncles again. Another girl. She was born two weeks before I left." He gave his brother a side glance and a smirk. "Papa wishes for a son."

Benjamin scoffed. "Not yet, little brother, not yet. But I'm glad there is another grandchild."

Jakob let the bellows rest to examine a broken wagon axle. He picked up an ax's handle in need of a head. "The work will go quicker if you let me help."

Benjamin nodded. "I do need the help and you'll be put to work soon enough. For now, just enjoy the rest." He removed the horseshoe and began working the metal.

Jakob cleared a place on the bench and sat down, leaning his head against the wall. Just to rest his eyes. That was all he needed. The rhythmic clanging lulled him. He was shaken awake a moment later with a start and looked around. His brother stood over him, amused.

"I was only resting my eyes for a few moments."

Benjamin chuckled. "A few moments? You were soundly sleeping, and it wasn't only for a few moments. Gather your things. Come. Tovah will be glad you arrived safely."

* * *

If Jakob's customer held the repaired chain any closer to his eyes, it would be inside his head. The man kept turning the links over and over, attempting to find any flaw, however minute, while Jakob stood passively in front of him, waiting to be paid. He knew his work was solid. He looked over at his brother, who was smiling.

Benjamin was clearly enjoying himself too much. He finally put his work aside to rescue Jakob. "I inspected his work. The chain will hold."

"Hmm. Perhaps. Perhaps not."

"Come now. There is no fault. Pay what is due."

The man looked straight at Benjamin and then at Jakob, reluctant to concede, before pulling out his purse and paying.

Jakob gave the coins to his brother and waited until the customer was far enough away not to overhear. "When will the customers trust my work?"

"Do you mean when will *my customers* trust your work?"

"You know what I say."

"It seemed an eternity before the townspeople could see that my work was just as good, if not better, than the old blacksmith's." He returned to examining the door latch that Jakob had finished just before the customer came for his chain. "Not bad. The hinges are next."

Jakob was about to reply, but then reluctantly looked for the hinges. No use getting into an argument.

Benjamin put down the repaired latch and pointed towards the workshop's doors. "In the sack, over by that barrel."

Jakob walked over, and, just as he was about to pick up the sack, he saw her: the beautiful girl he first saw when he was walking into town. He straightened and watched her. He was so amused that he almost laughed out loud when three village ruffians backed away from her. The three immediately diverted their attention, finding another young woman to taunt. Jakob took pity upon the woman. "You three! Let her be!"

The ruffians looked at Jakob, considering, and then moved away. The young woman gave Benjamin a slight smile in gratitude.

His eyes followed the beauty as she made her way towards the market.

"Benjamin! Come quickly!"

His brother was beside him in an instant. "What?! What happened?!" His eyes darted over Jakob for wounds and then beyond the doors of the workshop.

He pointed at the young woman who was talking to a woman he had seen after last Shabbot. "Who is she?"

"The woman?" The left side of Benjamin's mouth hitched in his "teasing" smile. "That's Rhea, the midwife."

Jakob wasn't in the mood for his brother's jests. "No, the younger one."

"Ah." He chuckled, shaking his head. "Don't concern yourself with her, little brother. She's Herr Nahon's niece, Anya. There are discussions for her betrothal."

His heart twisted. "Anya," he thought to himself. "Unusual name."

He saw how Benjamin was appraising him, and said, "I know that look."

"Her intended is the rabbanit's nephew."

His heart twisted a little more. One moment he was as gleeful as a young boy as he watched Anya fend off her would-be harassers; the next, he felt as if his body was sinking into the dirt up to his shins in despair. He couldn't take his eyes away from her.

"Tovah tells me the Nahon family is expecting her intended in two days for a special meal."

"What does this man do?" Jakob watched her bob a curtsey to the midwife and continue towards the market. He faced his brother.

"I hear that he's a clockmaker from a wealthy family. Rather, an apprentice to a clockmaker. I also hear he likes to make up-time clocks." Jakob had been hoping the man's employment was dangerous. "There are other fine young women here in Zaborstadt. Many fine beauties." His brother clapped him on his left shoulder. "There's work to be done."

* * *

"The hinges are finished and work is slow. I can deliver them." Jakob's offer sounded too eager to him, but he hoped Benjamin didn't notice.

"Would you now?" Benjamin's voice carried a speck of sarcasm. He looked up from his work and scoffed. "Or is it because you would pass the Nahon home?" It was more a statement than a question. Before anything else could be said, Jakob left with the hinges.

Jakob slowed when he approached the Nahon home. As he hoped, Anya was outside. She was sitting under a tree in front with a young boy he had learned was her cousin Simon. As he came closer, he saw that they held a slate between them. Simon wrote and pointed. Anya's brows creased in concentration, her mouth sounding out each word slowly, the boy helping her when she had trouble. Jakob stopped and watched. Simon looked up and nudged Anya with his right elbow. She stopped reading, and her head came up to scowl at Jakob. Then she shifted her seat around so that her back was to him. She made Simon do the same. Their shoulders were pinched, and their heads down.

Jakob blushed, looked down in embarrassment, and continued on to his delivery. At least he had seen Anya. The Nahons must truly be wealthy to be able to educate a girl! He barely knew how to read; he had never had any use for learning anything that didn't put money in his purse or food in his stomach.

* * *

The morning prayers were done and people were milling about outside. Jakob was half-listening to a man speaking with his brother about his horse needing a new shoe. He really couldn't care about horseshoes, chains, or wagon wheels. He watched Anya with Rahel and the midwife over the man's right shoulder. The man stopped talking and looked behind him. Rahel saw Jakob and was smiling with downcast, bashful eyes. He saw Anya frown and turn her back to him.

"Ah. Yes, Rahel." The man? Benjamin? faced Jakob. "Go ask her papa to court her."

"What?"

"She'll make a fine wife for you." He paused, appraising Jakob, then continued. "Rahel seems interested in you as well."

Jakob watched Anya give a quick bob and walk away. Rahel gave him her best possible smile.

Jakob rolled a newly repaired wagon wheel to its resting place with the other two. They had so many wheels to repair lately. *"How can I make a wheel that withstands the roads?"* He remembered one of his friends in his hometown showing him a drawing he had copied from an up-time book. *"If only I had examined the drawing more than watching the baker's daughter."*

"Jakob! Help me take this wheel off!" He turned around and saw Benjamin struggling. He was about to say something when a customer leading two horses entered the workshop. Benjamin stopped his efforts to remove a stubborn spoke from a wheel.

Jakob walked over to greet the man. "Good day, Herr Stein. I just finished your wheel. You have another that needs repair?"

Benjamin joined the two men. He took Herr Stein's horses to hitch them to the wagon.

Herr Stein looked around. "It seems I'm not the only one with such problems. Why is it that so many wheels are broken?"

"I inspected your wheel. The wood and metal. This is not my work. And not Jakob's." He said over his shoulder.

Stein was embarrassed. "No, not your work," then quickly added, not looking at Jakob, "Not your brother's."

"Another blacksmith's?" Jakob's question was an honest, inquisitive one. Benjamin shot him a side glance for him not to press further.

"Hmm."

Anya and Rahel passed by the shop. Jakob was immediately distracted. Rahel was animated in speaking while Anya appeared to be intently listening. His eyes followed Anya as she left Rahel, who had stopped to look at some apples, and went to the next stall to examine a basket. The stall's vendor came up to her and said something. Anya shook her head and put the basket back down. She left the stall and disappeared into the crowds. He wanted to run after her. Why did she make him act like a schoolboy?

Herr Stein chuckled. "Ah, I know that look well enough. A look that every young man has. Fine young woman, Rahel. Sturdy, obedient, and from a good, respectable family."

Jakob realized their customer was speaking to him. "What?"

"Rahel. I see that you fancy her. An excellent choice."

"I—" Why was everyone thinking that he was interested in Rahel?

Herr Stein interrupted. "She'll keep a good home and be a good mother to your children when the time comes. I understand from what my wife tells me she's already a very capable midwife. Unlike Anya." Shaking his head. "That one is a handful. Too high-spirited, my wife says. Cut her hair once and was told several times to cover her head. A proper young woman should already know to do this. Quite immodest. Must be that Spanish blood. Great misfortune follows that family—"

Jakob looked momentarily at his brother. Although his back was to them, he saw Benjamin's shoulders were hunched and the back of his neck red. Then he stopped hitching the horse on the right and turned. "Herr Stein, if the repair meets your satisfaction, please kindly pay what is due." Benjamin's interruption was terse.

Chastened, their customer took out his coin pouch. Based on what Jakob had seen of Anya, he couldn't understand how she was considered high-spirited. Or immodest. Jakob took the payment and helped his brother finish hitching the horses. The brothers were silent, waiting for Herr Stein to leave.

"He's just as bad as his gossiping wife," Benjamin said. They turned to go back to their work.

"Tovah is here with our midday meal." They watched Benjamin's wife, who was listening to Dora Nahon. Dora shook her head as she left her.

"Benjamin, Jakob." Tovah entered the shop.

"Wife! What did you bring us today?"

She lifted out a half-round of bread. "I also have some jam. And very sad news."

"Oh?" He took the bread and basket.

"Dora told me that Anya is no longer betrothed because of a lack of dowry from her father. She wanted to tell me herself, as word will quickly spread. She also said the rabbanit came to her home and apologized to Dora and Anya."

Jakob kept his expression neutral, but his heart was skipping in glee. In fact, this moment was the happiest he had been in a very long while. He took his share of the food in the basket and sat by himself with his elated thoughts while his brother and sister-in-law discussed common occurrences. Anya was no longer betrothed! He did his best not to smile.

* * *

Anya trudged through the open door after an afternoon of three visits administering care with Rahel and Rhea. Her feet hurt, her head hurt, she was hungry, and she was exhausted. She found everyone bent over a crate when she entered the home. They all looked at her.

"Come see, Anya! Come see!" Deborah ran up to her, pulling her to the center of the room where everyone was standing. Tio and Tia stepped aside for her to see a crate. They all looked at her eagerly.

"What is this?"

"It arrived today from your papa," said Tio. "We thought we would wait for your return."

"*I* thought we should wait for you to return," corrected Dora.

Danel gave his wife a side glance before prying the crate open and setting the lid against the side of the box.

Everyone looked inside. Anya unconsciously wiped her hands on her dirty apron and pushed some of the straw aside, to reveal plain, heavy, folded cloth and a letter from her Papa. Danel quickly snatched the letter and went to the hearth with Dora following him.

"See what's inside," Dora encouraged from her place by her husband's side. She positioned herself so that she could read over Danel's shoulder. Even before the seal was broken, she had really had no hope that Yeshua would provide for his daughter. Her brother-in-law wrote how his small son was thriving and happy. His wife was doing well managing the household and two servants. The final paragraph—all of three sentences—said that he was glad that Anya was betrothed to a fine young man, but in his financial circumstances he couldn't afford the funds for her dowry. Dora and Danel looked at one another with a mixture of disgust and disappointment.

Anya's attention wasn't on her tio and tia. She reached in and drew out her mother's green dress with the silver embroidery.

"It's beautiful." Roza traced a silver design with her index finger.

At first, Anya didn't know what to make of this. Why would he give her the dress? Did his horrid second wife not want it? Most likely that was so.

"Look, there's something else," Roza reached in to retrieve another bundle, but Simon grabbed her arm and shook his head. "Leave this to Anya." The girl took a step back.

Anya unwrapped the second bundle and found a pair of embroidered shoes and a pendant made of carved shell on a velvet cord. These also belonged to her mother and were not as valuable as her other shoes or jewelry. Anya suspected that her stepmother had kept those for herself. She should have at least received one of her mother's strands of pearls.

Anya turned to her tio and tia and knew even before she asked what was written. "What did Papa say?" She held tightly to her hope. "Will he send the dowry for me?" They both looked at her, disappointed. Tia's expression was mixed with anger. The room was unbearably silent, but Anya still held onto the tiny speck of hope.

"My dear," Danel said slowly, "Your papa is very glad for your betrothal." He took a breath, "but he doesn't have the funds for your dowry. He sent the dress, shoes, and jewelry for your wedding. They were your mother's."

Disgust, then rage rose to her cheeks. "I don't want them."

"Why not?" Dora asked. "These were your mother's. I remember her wearing them."

She dropped the bundle back in the crate. "Get rid of the lot!" She ran out, but not before she overheard her tia say, "We'll keep them for her."

She was so furious, she slapped a nearby tree and immediately regretted doing so. She shook her hand in pain and muffled a yelp. Then she kicked the tree because her hand was hurting. She kicked the tree again because she hated her stepmother. It was all that woman's fault that she didn't have a dowry, that Papa had cast her aside. That was the truth of the matter. She knew it. She wanted to go back to her secret place in the woods, but she didn't want to. She slapped the tree with her other hand (much gentler this time). She paced back and forth, cursing her stepmother under her breath. She balled up her fists at her sides. The pain fed her anger. She wished the woman was here now. She would strike *her* instead of a tree.

"Anya?" It was a gentle question filled with concern from a small voice. Hearing her name caused her to stop her pacing and helped settle her. She turned around and looked at Simon.

"Leave me. Go back inside."

He scuffed a bare foot in the dirt and looked down. Then he met her eyes. "I'm glad you're staying."

She stared at her cousin and thought for a few moments. "I know you are."

"Would you like being married and living so far away?"

She was about to reply. She had to think about this. Did Simon think she was angry because she was no longer betrothed? Did she really want to be married to Efraim? She didn't even know him. But that was the way things were done. Would she learn to love him? Would he truly allow her to become a nurse? "I don't know." Her cousin's question calmed her rage. She went back inside with Simon.

It took only one week. She did her best to ignore the stolen glances and the "tsk-tsking" with her chin forward and set and an emotionless expression when she went about in the market. After that, she refused to leave home and kept herself occupied with her many chores. She had been abandoned by her father and discarded by her betrothed. There were times when her mind raced and she had to run off to her place in the woods so that she could cry in private.

Anya was down to an occasional snuffle during one ugly bout of crying. She wiped her eyes with her apron and listened. A rustling noise was getting closer to her secret place. Lucky for her that she was sitting amidst the protection of thick pines and bramble. She flattened herself on the ground as if she were a scared rabbit and carefully, quietly crawled mere inches to the edge of her hiding place to see what was making such a lumbering noise. She hoped it wasn't a hungry predator.

Worse!

It was that ox of an awful young man—Jakob—gathering flowers. So, he was the one leaving her the flowers! The gall of him. Before her self-imposed isolation, he was there every time she went to market and at synagogue after services. Now he was *here*! How dare he come so close to her place!? She wanted to be left alone in her heartbreak. She scooted back as quickly and quietly as she was able, to hide, but still be able to watch him. She waited for him to leave and then got up, brushing the pine needles from her clothes.

"Anya, it's been a month, and it's time to show yourself." Tia placed a hand gently on hers so that she stopped scrubbing the long-gone stain from a shirt. She turned her head to look at her tia. "I'm worried for you. We all are." Anya didn't say anything. "I think going to synagogue would be good."

"I don't want to go." She resumed her scrubbing.

Dora sighed and took the shirt away, examining the cloth for signs of damage. "You'll ruin this." She set it down in the washtub. "You must not allow gossip to get the better of you. The shame is not yours."

"Efraim is not here. I am. They see me. I see and hear how everyone accuses me."

Her tia looked at her, knowing what she said was true. "But you are becoming a very capable midwife. And you know how to make remedies. Something that you should be proud of."

A few days later, Anya stared at the back of the butcher's wife's head while sitting absolutely still and straight in the women's section. She held her head forward, chin up, hoping that her posture looked stoic even while her insides churned in chaos. Tovah sat on her left, occasionally giving her hand a reassuring pat and smiling at her when Anya looked her way. Tia was on her right, making sure their shoulders touched. Anya sat as still and straight as she was able, thinking the posture would help keep her turmoil from surfacing. It was no surprise to her that she could still hear the hushed gossiping and the "tsk-tsking". *"Such shame for the family, they're truly not favored." "Of all people, the rabbi's nephew." " What will the Nahons do now?" "Who will marry the girl?" " Wasn't it such a pity for Herr Nahon's niece?" "What will become of her?"* Anya turned her head very slightly and saw how concerned Tia was for her. She returned a half-hearted smile. She wanted to leave. Now. She continued staring at the back of the butcher's wife's head while Tia made her three restless children behave.

The prayers were excruciatingly long, but they could finally go outside when they ended.

"Tio is over there with Benjamin and Tovah. Come." They followed Dora. Anya caught sight of Jakob, who was making his way to his brother and sister-in-law. She was in no mood to exchange pleasantries with the tree-stump-for-a-head ox.

Anya interrupted. "Please, Tio. I want to go home now."

"Do you have a need?" Tia Dora tapped his arm and gave him one of her expressions. "Of course."

"Children, go with Anya."

Anya wanted to run—escape—from the side-long glances and whispers. She fought the impulse; with her head slightly tilted down to avoid any eye contact, she took Deborah by the hand, and led Simon and Roza away. At least she wouldn't add to the gossip by crying.

She constantly thought about going to Grantville: while she did her chores, while she was learning how to prepare medicines and poultices, and while she was assisting Rhea alongside Rahel.

She was tending to the garden. Her daydreams took over her thoughts. What would happen if Efraim came down the road? She could see him walking purposefully towards her. He had come to beg for forgiveness and to ask her to marry him. Her hoe exposed a worm. The corners of her mouth turned up slightly as she brought the hoe down and crushed it. "You are mad to think that I would wed someone like you! Go make your up-time clocks! See if I care! Leave me be!" She surprised herself when she spoke aloud. She would become a midwife and live in Simon's household when the time came. Never to marry and have her own children. That was her fate.

Benjamin stopped his hammering when he saw Jakob shuffle into the shop, head down, shoulders slumped, and sullen. "Tell me." He stepped around the anvil to stand in front of his brother.

"I gave the flowers to Simon and told him to give them to Anya. Then I went to the other side of the road and hid."

"And?"

"Anya came out and fed the flowers to the goats and chickens. Just like last time."

Benjamin laughed. It was a from-the-belly laugh that made him bend over and slap his legs. He straightened with one final guffaw. "Just like last time! Little brother, just go ask Danel if you may court Anya."

"He'll say 'no'."

"You don't know this. I know my friend and he knows you're a good man."

Jakob didn't say anything else. He picked up an old discarded horseshoe and threw it in the pile that would eventually be melted and made into other things. The horseshoe landed with a clang, causing a long nail to roll out of the pile. Jakob stared at it and got an idea. He thought about his idea all through his tasks that afternoon. He would rise early the next day.

* * *

Dora looked up from her endless mending when she heard the door slam. Her husband was holding a bouquet and something else she couldn't quite make out. "More flowers, I see. From Jakob, I presume."

"Yes, and this." He opened his palm. Dora leaned forward. It was two long nails entwined in the shape of a heart.

"Hmm." She took it to examine the handiwork. "It's very nice."

Anya entered. Her eyes narrowed in disgust when she saw the flowers, knowing very well who they were from. "He's an oaf. And they mean nothing to me. I'll feed them to the animals."

"He gave you this as well." Dora held out the nail-entwined heart for her.

She frowned. "I need to fetch water." She picked up a bucket by the stand and dishpan and left.

Danel sat down at the table. "What happened? Doesn't she realize that Jakob is smitten with her?"

"I'm sure she does." She handed her husband the token. "Jakob will make a fine husband for her. He's earnest, steadfast, and hard-working. Go to

Benjamin and invite him for supper next Shabbot. And Tovah and Jakob as well."

"What?"

She looked up at the ceiling in exasperation. Her husband could be so half-witted at times. "Speak to Benjamin. Discuss Jakob's courtship with Anya and invite them all after Shabbot. What say you?"

"Would this be agreeable to Anya? You see how she is."

"I remember how you approached my father before we courted. He agreed quickly enough."

Danel's family was well off and had belonged to the Church although they were secretly Jewish, as was her family. She had learned to love him in time. He never raised a hand to her, and he allowed her to speak her mind: both rarities. Dora smiled. Anya was another matter. The girl was headstrong and was even influenced by up-time thought and customs. She was also heartsick and melancholy.

"He doesn't have a home of his own."

"He will. You'll recall that you didn't have a home of your own when we courted."

"And his employment?" He regretted the words as soon as he said them.

Her left eyebrow cocked and the left side of her mouth raised. "What of it? Aren't you in the employ of your brother?"

He mumbled, looking down at his feet. "I'll speak to Benjamin and I'll ask Jakob his intentions."Jakob saw Danel come into the shop and looked over at Benjamin. His brother jerked his head to Danel and Jakob understood that he should be the one to speak to their customer.

"Herr Nahon, good day. What are we able to do for you?"

"Jakob, good day." He paused. The man's expression and posture made Jakob feel uncomfortable. Even more so when he said, "It has come to my attention that you are interested in my niece. Is this true?"

Jakob hastily took out a dirty rag tucked in his leather apron and wiped his hands as a way to stall. "I— I—"

"Well, what are your intentions?"

Jakob looked over at Benjamin, who was trying not to laugh as he turned his back and walked away. How did he know? Jakob looked back to Danel. "I want to court Anya."

"Good. Come to my home after Shabbot with Tovah and Benjamin. In the afternoon. We will discuss this matter further." He turned and left. Jakob stood there staring at the retreating man making his way through the bustle of the street.

"Little brother, close your mouth before you catch flies."

"I must be sure my good shirt is freshly laundered."

"You should have no worries about that. Tovah saw to it already."

He looked at Benjamin. "How did she know?"

Benjamin's answer was a toothy grin and chuckle. He went back to his work.

* * *

Anya yelled, "NO!" pounding the table with her left fist as she stood.

"What?" Danel was surprised. He thought she would be glad. Dora and the children were silent, looking at one another.

"I'm not a horse that can be traded at will! I won't be married!" She stomped out of the house, the door slamming in her wake. Everyone jumped in their seats at the sound.

Dora was the first to speak. "She's a Nahon. Defiant. Strong-willed."

Danel wanted to say something, but he thought it better not to argue now.

"I'll go speak with her." Dora stood.

"No, wife," he said. He stood, took his towel from his left shoulder, and set it down by his plate. "I will."

Dora stood up as if to join him, but he waved his right hand down in a gesture for her to sit.

As Danel reached the door, he heard Simon ask, "If she marries the blacksmith's brother, will she stay in Zaborstadt?" The last thing he heard was Dora telling him to finish eating.

The latch clicked in place.

Anya was standing by the well, looking down at the blackness. "Anya?" he asked as he approached her.

She didn't bother turning to face him or even look over her shoulder. "Leave me."

"This I cannot do." He stood beside her. "Why are you opposed to marriage? You seemed so happy with your betrothal to Efraim."

"Tio, I was happy with Efraim because we would live in Grantville. I would go to the nursing school. Simon is teaching me how to read."

"Ah, I see." There was sympathy in his eyes. "Give Jakob a chance. He'll be good to you."

* * *

Anya was asked to check the lamb stew she was preparing for Benjamin, Tovah, and Jakob. Her best dish. The same one she served for Efraim and his aunt and uncle. She was forced to prepare it, as she was forced to wash her hair and bathe from head to toe. It wasn't the week for her to wash her hair and she had already bathed, but she had to do it again, anyway. She wanted to rub ash in her freshly laundered skirt and apron. What silliness, all this preparation.

Simon popped his head in the open door. "Mama, they're coming down the road now!"

Dora finished wiping the table. "Ah, good. Tell Papa we'll be out to join him. Make sure Deborah and Roza are there. Come, Anya."

She would much rather run to her place in the woods than greet the guests. She stood to the right and slightly behind her tio and tia while her cousins clustered behind their parents.

Danel, smiling warmly, walked to the guests as they approached. "Welcome!"

Anya stepped back to where her cousins were standing.

Benjamin and Jakob bowed and Tovah bobbed. Jakob looked awkward, holding a bouquet of flowers. Anya wanted to kiss the top of Simon's head when she saw him scowling at Jakob. She smiled in appreciation at her cousin instead. When she looked at Jakob, she noticed he was nervous; probably from Simon scowling at him.

"I—," he said. "This is for Anya."

"Of course." Danel turned to his niece. "Anya, Jakob has flowers for you."

Dora came forward. "How very thoughtful." She looked at Anya who remained in place by her cousins. "Anya," she said gently. Anya didn't move. Her aunt shifted her eyes and nodded to Jakob. She still didn't move. Then more forcefully, "Anya, please put the flowers in a pitcher of water and set them on the table."

Jakob clumsily thrust the bouquet in front of her. She was reluctant to obey, but she took the flowers. They were held together by a long blade of grass. She mumbled, "Thank you," while looking down at the ground.

"I picked them along the way."

"Let Jakob and me speak in private for a moment, if you don't mind, Benjamin. Then we will join you. Children, go play," Danel said.

Anya's cousins quickly ran off before Benjamin replied.

"Not at all. I'll wait here."

* * *

It was easy for Anya to conclude what the conversation between Jakob and Tio might be.

"Tovah, please come inside with Anya and me."

"Of course." Tovah followed the two.

Anya filled a pitcher with water and dumped the flowers in it, ignoring the disapproval from Tia as she set them in the center of the table.

Tovah noticed the tension. Wanting to quell the mood, she said, "The flowers look lovely on the table," then softly chuckled. "I must tell you Jakob was so nervous earlier. He forgot to tie his cuffs before he put his shirt on and Benjamin had to help him tie them. He was so nervous that Benjamin even had to comb beeswax in his hair. His hands were shaking so."

"He looks especially handsome." Looking at Anya. "Don't you think so, niece mine?"

Anya understood just by her tia's encouraging tone what response was expected. "Yes. Handsome." She answered just a little too flatly.

Her tia looked at her with her signature narrowed eyes, tight lips, and we-will-discuss-this-later scowl.

Tovah looked at the hearth. "It smells wonderful!" She said, intervening.

"Anya's best dish," Dora said.

"Lamb stew. We had it for Efraim, the rabbi, and rabbanit." Anya said. Tia's head snapped at her, reproving. Again.

"Isn't that the token that Jakob made for you, Anya?" Tovah asked, looking at the heart made from two nails. It was propped up on the mantle over the hearth.

Anya hated that her tia had hidden it from her before she could discard it and then had even put it on display for today's visit.

Before anything else could be said, the door opened and Danel came in, followed by Benjamin and Jakob and Anya's cousins. Tio and Benjamin were laughing. Benjamin patted Jakob on his left shoulder in good humor.

"I must say to all, it is agreed that Anya will be betrothed to Jakob for one year. Within that one year, Jakob is to provide a home for them on the day of their wedding. He's a fine blacksmith and will continue to be in his brother's employ. It will be a wonderful day when our two families are joined."

Dora gave Anya an affectionate hug. "Wonderful day, this is!"

Anya hoped he would never be able to provide a house for her.

Tovah clasped her hands to her chest in glee. "Husband, we must tell your parents at once."

"Of course, of course."

"First, let us wash our hands and have a fine meal."

Simon, who until that moment was sullen, had a huge smile. He went to Benjamin and took his hand with both of his. Benjamin's hand was so huge that it seemed to swallow the boy's hands. "Come. This way." And he started to lead him to the pitcher and bowl. "Do you know the prayer? I do. I can help you."

When they passed the hearth on their left, Jakob noticed the token and looked at Anya with the corners of his mouth curled slightly, appreciating the gesture. She wanted to tell him she had never cared for the gift. Instead, she cast her eyes down and looked impassive.

Once everyone had washed his or her hands, Dora instructed their guests where to sit. Anya saw that Jakob would be sitting on her left. She was not happy with this arrangement.

One of the serving bowls had recently been broken, so Tia and Anya remained at the hearth, ladling the meat with gravy and vegetables onto plates to be served one at a time.

"Please prepare Jakob's dish and then your own." Tia placed her dish and Anya's on the table and then went to wash her hands.

Anya quickly glanced over her right shoulder being sure that everyone at the table was occupied in conversation. She looked back at the pots. She picked up the empty plate using her skirt and apron. She actually was using her clothing as a shield. She ladled meat and gravy, and sprinkled a healthy amount of salt on to the plate. Bending her knees slightly, she used an extra spoon in an old clay tankard by the hearth and scooped up ash, then mixed the "enhanced" version as soundlessly as possible. Last, she plopped a careless dollop of vegetables on top of the meat. It was her hope that once he discovered she was a poor cook, he would quickly ask that she not be his intended. She returned to Jakob's side, giving him a wide smile, mischievous while serving him his helping. He returned the smile. He was such a fool.

"Let us bless this meal," Danel said. When he finished reciting the prayer, he added, "Please enjoy."

"Anya made the meat and gravy dish. As you all know, Anya is a wonderful cook. You'll see when you taste it." Tia Dora beamed. She said this since Benjamin and Jakob didn't know.

Anya gave her a half-smile. She had to admit this meal was much more relaxed than the one with Efraim and the rabbi and rabbanit. "I'm going to learn nursing. In Grantville." Everyone looked at her. Tia Dora shook her head very slightly. This time her lips almost disappeared in her disapproval.

Jakob coughed into a dirty rag that he used as his handkerchief.

Anya suppressed a smile, knowing the real reason why he was coughing.

"Jakob, there's no need to worry. Anya will come to see that being a good wife and mother to your children is just the thing."

"Of course, Herr Nahon."

Anya watched him, smiling, as he ate a spoonful of ash and overly salted stew. Her smile was a little too self-satisfied.

"Anya will be a fine midwife. There will be no need for her to be a nurse," offered Tia Dora.

No, she wasn't going to be a good wife to him! Anya thought. It took a lot of will to keep herself from not gleefully giggling.

"Is business doing well?" Asked Benjamin.

"Very much so." Danel discussed this topic for a good part of the evening.

Anya saw that every so often, Jakob would "cough" and place another piece of meat in his handkerchief. It amused her that he actually thought no one at the table noticed this. Yet, she was amazed that he managed to choke the vegetables down.

The shadows were very long on their way home.

"Tell me, little brother, now that you've met Anya, what do you say?"

Jakob was quick to respond. "She's very shy. Never even looked at me once in public. But she has a pretty smile, I learned tonight."

Benjamin and Tovah nodded in appreciation. Jakob slowed so that he could walk a few paces behind the couple. The real reason he walked behind them was not so they could hold a conversation between the two of them, but so that he could casually throw a piece of the awful meat in the grass on the side of the road as they went. Every so often he would look behind him for the bits of meat left behind. If that was Anya's best dish, then he would be a very thin husband indeed. He felt guilty when he envisioned some poor scavenging creature becoming sick shortly after eating the offering. Maybe it would have been better to simply bury the remains instead.

* * *

Anya was in a foul mood the day after the visit and meal and the next two days while tending to her visits with Tia, then with Rhea and Rahel. On the third day, Anya passed the blacksmith's shop on the way to market without even looking at Jakob. It was his fault that she would never have the chance to learn to read and become a nurse. Deep in her thoughts, she didn't see a ruffian come up and "accidently" bump into her with a smirk and snicker.

Anya turned around just as Jakob ran out and grabbed the street urchin by the back of the neck. The boy's feet barely touched the ground as Jakob dragged him by the back of his shirt and right arm to Anya where she gawked. People nearby stopped to watch, point, and laugh.

Jakob shook him as if he were getting the dust out of a filthy towel, yelling, "You dare to accost my beloved and intended?!" He shook the struggling boy again. "Apologize!"

She looked at him appreciatively. Maybe Jakob did have some redeeming qualities after all. She would give him a chance.

Antwerp Antics

John Deakins

Antwerp

1636

Anthony Van Dyck was happy, but nervous. Things were going extremely well. Still, he kept waiting for the next black cloud to billow over the horizon. Antwerp was blooming like a springtime rose. King Ferdinand wouldn't allow the Inquisition to establish itself in Antwerp again. Instead of being an uneasy fringe cabal, artists of every type were flocking there.

That was no surprise for the Low Countries or Holland, since the Spanish and the Dutch war had ended. The *Dutch School* and the *Flemish School* would soon merge. French artists appeared regularly in the port city. The uncertain French succession and a hovering war with the USE kept artists continually jittery. King Gaston wasn't as bad as King Charles, but he was unpredictable. Antwerp seemed welcoming by comparison.

The Americans had their fingers in everything. They'd helped King Ferdinand to find his lovely wife, encouraged him to assume the Spanish Netherlands throne, and to make peace and common cause with the Dutch. Their *future history* had described how a frustrating English project would have destroyed Anthony's own health. The *date of his future death* was now meaningless. At age thirty-seven, he was at the top of his form, in nearly ideal health. That could be traced to American insistence on clean water and uncontaminated food. Van Dyck had adopted his name's American spelling, though the English spelled it three or four different ways.

Even better, he'd made peace with his old mentor, Peter-Paul Rubens. Rubens' death had also been postponed by American medical help. Still, his friend was showing his age. Rubens no longer took every project offered him. He concentrated on landscapes, but he still took commissions for religious Counter-Reformation art and classical paintings. Rubens had tired of the effort needed to portray royalty, nobles, and wealthy merchants. He'd thrown that field open to Van Dyck.

Anthony didn't jest with himself. In 1636, he was the best European portrait painter alive. His grandfather and his great-uncle had been well-known artists. Anthony had been a teen prodigy with the paintbrush. His teachers in Antwerp and Italy had been respected artists. He was better than any of them. He'd been the English royal family's court artist, painting forty portraits of Charles and thirty of Henrietta Maria. On paper, he'd been well paid for his art. Charles I had a habit of putting off Anthony's £200 stipend indefinitely, paying only slowly for portraits. Other nobles' portraits had kept him well off.

That life was over. He'd returned to Antwerp, the city of his birth. King Charles had been mildly insane since Doctor William Harvey had slipped him a copy of his own *future history.* Maddened further by his wife's death, the English king had become a bomb with a sputtering fuse. His mercenaries were hunting down men who'd never done him harm.

They'd someday, in a future that no longer existed, rebel against him. He was turning England on its head, creating the very revolt that he'd tried to suppress.

Van Dyck felt good, but guilty, that he'd helped spirit Europe's best engraver out of unstable England. After Vosterman had engraved Van Dyck's whole *Iconography*, he'd convinced the engraver to move to England, to duplicate Van Dyck's portraits and to stay away from Rubens in Antwerp. There'd been fading bad blood between the two. The older engraver's eyesight was weakening, but American-inspired eyeglasses had slowed the process.

Vosterman had two promising students, his apprentice son, twelve-year-old Lucas, and journeyman engraver Giorgio Fabrini. Fabrini's strange past had caused his family to escape Italian chaos. The Italian Pope, under the Spanish thumb, had to compete with the original, escaped Pope, under his own control, far from Italy. Which way Italy's future would jump was conjectural. Stable men were creeping out of the Italian boot with whatever they could carry. Italian artists were turning up in Antwerp. Because of six years in Italy, Anthony could converse with Fabrini and other Italians. Fabrini also spoke English.

Van Dyck wore his chin beard like a badge. He probably always would, since the Americans had shown him the future beard style would bear his name. He had a fine Antwerp house, the same *Stadt van Ghent* he'd lived in as a teen. Like other Antwerp homes during the past repression, it had been neglected. He had the wherewithal to repair it. Customers came to Antwerp, just to employ him. He might never have to travel again, unless the money was right. It would have to be *very* right. Everything was going well.

Why, then, was he uneasy?

* * *

Two ships docked in Antwerp from English ports. The harbor was so busy that arrivals were barely news. Passengers had been crowded into every space. Van Dyck and Vosterman weren't alone in leaving England. Van Dyck, busy with a portrait of Maria Anna, the Queen of the Spanish Netherlands, paid the arrivals no mind. Sometimes you miss the oncoming storm until it's too late to take cover.

Days later, comfortable in the *Stadt van Ghent*, Van Dyck had a visitor. His butler announced, "Lady Margaret Lemon."

Anthony muttered to himself, "Dear God, what have I done to deserve this? Lady? I don't think so!"

He rose sharply as the well-dressed woman swept into the room. At age twenty-two, her fine features showed only minimal wear and tear. At middle age, his bodily scuffing had delved deeper. She was powerfully familiar to him. She'd been beautiful when she modeled for him, the most in-demand *commoner* model in England. She'd been his mistress and his partner. He wasn't the first artist to sample her affections. They had a mutual history. He'd planned to leave her, and that history, behind in England.

"Have you been well, Margaret?" He bent to kiss her hand, as if she were really a *Lady*. He waved her to a comfortable chair.

"Well enough." She settled in a swirl of skirts. "I'll not ask how you're doing, Anthony. You have this great house. Everything about you shouts, 'Money!' Did your feet catch fire on their flight from England? Your English workshop's employees are either dead, turned to robbery, or beggars. You left me without a good-bye, with no income and your property to look after." She flicked her reddish blonde hair.

"As I recall, your tastes would have diminished any coin I left behind in a dazzlingly short time. What happened to *Blackfriars?*"

"Alas, I had to sell it. An earl—Don't ask—took over it, and me. I eventually squeezed enough gold out of him to bribe my way out of England. I've enough to live well here, at least temporarily. He didn't get the bargain in *Blackfriars* that he'd anticipated. I'd sold off everything I could. The mansion was shabby to the point that he'll need plenty to refurbish it. It needed your income and my management."

"Hmmm. You're in Antwerp. Now what?"

"I haven't lost my looks. I can still model. Perhaps Rubens could place me in some sylvan scene. He seems to prefer models with more flesh on them, but there are many artists in Antwerp. I'll find work." An image flickered in his mind of Margaret standing nude as a *chaste Venus.*

"Yes, I'm sure that you will." Anthony van Dyck wasn't who he was by being slow on his feet. A new design leaped into his head, full blown. "Are you as musically talented as always?"

She raised her eyebrows as she looked down her nose. "I'm probably as good as ever. Why do you ask?"

He steepled his fingers. "A thought has occurred to me. I have this house in adequate shape. I don't like my gold sitting in a bank, waiting for someone else to invest it. I'm buying the *Kasteel van Rijssel*, the house where my mother died. There'll soon be a housing shortage in Antwerp. The city is becoming a Mecca, since neither war nor the Inquisition are at our doorstep. Certainly the house has deteriorated. I know what you did at *Blackfriars.* You're staying at an inn?"

"Yes. The *Goulen Piramide.* Why?"

"Why don't you move to the *Kasteel van Rijssel*? Repair it. Manage it. Hire the right servants. I know you can do it."

"Hmmph. I'll think about it. What's in it for me?" Her face would have modeled a portrait for *The Spirit of Skepticism.*

"You'll live rent free. You'll start out in Antwerp with a blank slate among creditors. Have the renovation bills sent to me. You'd refurnish your own quarters first, of course. Add an artist's studio. My grandfather painted there. I might sometimes work there. Other artists could come to you to model in your own residence. I don't know about you, but I've had my fill of long journeys."

She frowned. "What—What you say is interesting. I'm worried, though. What we had before involved some, ah, sexual strings. Since you abandoned me in England, I'm not sure I want to tie those strings again." Her current arrival in his presence softened her final statement.

"You're still a handsome woman. Who knows what might happen in the future? That's not part of this arrangement. I need you as a business partner and a manager, instead of a bed partner." Contrasting emotions flickered across her face. "Once the new house is prospering, build a music room with a harpsichord. I plan to entertain there, from time to time. This house will be my main studio and my retreat. Perhaps I'll occasionally have a few guests here. I'd appreciate it if you could mingle with my guests as my hostess. Perhaps play for them on the recorder. What do you think?"

He had the plan. It was such a positive idea, sprung on her without warning, that it overwhelmed her. "I—I don't know."

"Why not return to the *Goulen Piramide* and think it over? I'll meet you for an evening dinner tomorrow about sunset. Tell me your decision then." She didn't notice that she was being gentled out the door. Not exactly the *bum's rush*, it still delivered her to the street rapidly. Her carriage driver hadn't finished his tobacco pipe. She departed, with wheels clattering on cobbles.

Anthony van Dyck plopped into his chair. Sweat had soaked his armpits. He'd never been interested in warfare. Nevertheless, he felt that Fate's arrow had just missed him. He breathed a sigh of relief. Margaret would be across town. He could control his access to her and her access to him. She'd certainly cheat him on the house renovation. Margaret always liked spending better than saving. He knew it, and she knew that he knew it. Still, she managed *Blackfriars* so well that her skimming had never interfered with its operation.

He sighed again, unaware that Fate had more than one arrow in his quiver.

* * *

Lady Mary Ruthven was a doctor's daughter. Though a commoner, he loved to style himself *Lord Ruthven.* Mary, as much a commoner as her father, had indeed been a *Lady*, because she was a lady-in-waiting for Queen Henrietta Maria. As long as she served in that post, she was a *Lady*, no matter her origins.

Unfortunately, Queen Henrietta Maria was dead, killed in a carriage accident. That left Mary Ruthven's position floating in limbo. Negotiations had begun by the queen for her engagement to Sir Anthony van Dyck, the court painter. He'd promised her a betrothal portrait. Within a few years, they'd have married. Both had enough status and income that their *court* marriage should have been successful. She wasn't an ugly woman. Waiting the years through the betrothal negotiations wouldn't have improved her looks.

Now, she felt as if her life's ship was foundering under her. Like her own status, England was in chaos. Her future was an unfinished, unraveling tapestry. She needed to get away. There were few places to run. She had jewelry the late queen had given her. A few other pieces had stuck to her hand. She still lived in the palace, but it was only a matter of time until King Charles' flunkies struck her from their *monetary support* ledger.

Her father was dithering, sucking up to the new elite. She had to act independently. In a dream, the sun rose over Antwerp and Sir Anthony van

Dyck. He'd been moving sluggishly toward marrying her *someday*. That *almost-future* needed to be reestablished. Only she could accomplish that.

Pawning some jewelry, she'd found a ship's captain in Bournemouth, awed enough by her *Ladyship* and her Ladyship's money to carry her to Antwerp. The ship had been crowded. It stank, but the Netherlands were only days away. The same day Margaret Lemon disembarked, Mary Ruthven arrived aboard *King Henry Ninth* in Antwerp harbor. She found minimal accommodations and began to plan.

* * *

Anthony van Dyck had created a distance buffer between him and Margaret Lemon. She'd gone readily for the chance to manage another house for him. Their relationship remained touchy. That made him feel *safer*. Permanent *safety* would exist only through constant vigilance. On guard against his cross-city former mistress, he was ambushed. The next blind-side slammed into him.

His butler called, "Master, Lady Mary Ruthven is here to see you." (Was his servant smirking?)

Anthony had changed his perspiration-soaked clothes only days before. Cold sweat ruined another set. Another problem that should have stayed in England had migrated to his door. Whatever that woman wanted would only cause him discomfort. He looked at the ceiling. "Dear God, what next? Will pitchforks and rabbits begin falling from the sky?" He shook his head. "Oh, show her in! Show her in."

She was wearing a court dress, like the ones in which he'd seen her in the queen's presence. She swept into the room, with the grace she'd learned in a royal court. He could only bow over her hand and offer her his finest chair. He ordered the butler to bring wine for two. He'd successfully hustled Margaret Lemon out the door without even a glass of ale. This *Lady* was from a different background. She wore nobility like a shawl.

Wearing the face she'd have presented to the king himself, she accepted the wine. "How is your health, Sir Anthony?" A commoner had to learn to speak precise, courtly English in royalty's presence.

"I'm physically excellent. And yourself?" *Sir* Anthony. He'd stopped using the honorific bestowed by King Charles. It reminded him of a life he preferred as a distant memory.

She sipped the wine. "I'm in fine fettle. You seem to be the same, and I am pleased. Do you see any of our old acquaintances here in Antwerp?" Barely past age twenty, she was indeed in fine fettle.

"No. Surprisingly few. The ones who arrive tend to continue to Paris or Amsterdam, or to the American enclave at Grantville. Artists stay here, but those seeking political favor want to be closer to the sources of power. How do things flow in England?"

She grimaced. "Things are in a bloody flux. (Pardon the crude pun.) Some you knew have been elevated. Some have been arrested. Some, disgraced and suppressed. A few have been killed. The mercenaries the king brought in keep a kind of order in London, but they do so in the crudest possible way." She shook her head and sipped her wine again. There was a silence between them.

He broke first. "What brings you to Antwerp?"

She'd been thinking about her answer for days. "We met at court. I've always found you handsome enough, a person of quality. I'd hoped that you found me the same"—Never mind that their engagement had been the queen's idea—"Your representative and my father had begun negotiations for a betrothal."

All that was true. She was a handsome woman, in her prime, much younger than him. He and she were elevated commoners, with *elevated* the key word. It had appeared to be an ideal arranged marriage. He could hardly have asked Margaret Lemon to be his agent, to arrange a marriage to another woman. Van Dyck had had his attorney begin the matter.

"With conditions as they are, I wasn't certain—"

"In your absence, your attorney completed the arrangements. Unfortunately, my patroness, the queen, died, and your attorney was accused of plotting against the king. He's in Newgate Prison, I hear. Nevertheless, you and I are betrothed, engaged to be married. Those silly *future history* books would have us married in 1640, but life is chaotic. It needs to be sooner." Fabrication came to members of the English court as spring leaves come to a forest.

Van Dyck's head had begun to spin, a condition that could only worsen. "You came to the Netherlands on your own? What—?"

"My father is afraid to move too far from the court, lest in his absence he be charged with treason by enemies. Remember your attorney." She'd long rehearsed her story. It even sounded reasonable to her. "He felt that I'd be safer out of England." That was true, except for the sentence's subject. Her father had ignored her for weeks. He could no longer count on her connection to the queen.

Her words struck him like a stone from the sky. He knew he looked foolish, like a gasping trout on a stream bank. "My dear," he said, immediately regretting his choice of words. "Uh, my dear, you realize that you've given me a great deal to think about."

"Yes, I suppose so. The facts speak for themselves. I'm staying at the *Three Oaks Inn*. They speak English there. I hope to see a great deal of you in the near future." She rose, clearly signaling departure.

He leaped to his feet, trying for decorum, with his liver roaring. She advanced on him. He tried not to flinch as she gave him the smallest of kisses on his lips. His butler opened the front door, and she swept out. A *Lady* knows how to exit a room.

Sir Anthony van Dyck flopped back into his chair. "Hankins!"

"Yes, Herr Van Dyck?"

"The wine you opened for Lady Ruthven and myself—Bring me the whole bottle. No more visitors today."

"Yes, Herr Van Dyck." Hankins was smirking again. Other servants, from nearby mansions, would find the Van Dyck goings-on the juiciest of gossip.

* * *

Anthony van Dyck liked the engraver Giorgio Fabrini. The young man had great potential. With Vosterman teaching him, he bridged the gap between the older engraver and his still-developing son. The three should become the go-to engravers for all Europe in the decades ahead. No mean engraver himself, Van Dyck knew good work when he saw it. He'd paid a research expert to search the Grantville library for information about Vosterman's life.

The tough old bird would outlive Anthony, but without help, he'd have died blind and poor thirty years in the future. At the moment, he wasn't producing much work since his wife had died. She'd been sickly. The research said she'd died in 1642, after Van Dyck's own scheduled death. Instead, trying to slip out of England quietly, she'd ingested bad food or water. She'd died aboard ship, never seeing Antwerp. Her children had sheltered with Van Dyck until the older Vosterman arrived.

On paper, Van Dyck owned Vosterman's engraving studio but that was an investment. As soon as the engraver began turning out metal copies of Van Dyck's own portraits, he'd be able to pay back the loan. In the meantime, both Vosterman and Fabrini owed Anthony a large payback.

Van Dyck had invited both Peter-Paul Rubens and Giorgio Fabrini for dinner at his home. He needed advice. He'd already investigated some non-solutions of his problems. He loved Italy. Getting out of town on an extended *road trip* had seemed like a good idea. Unfortunately, Italy was experiencing dangerous turmoil. France under Gaston might be at war soon. Spain hated anything to do with Antwerp. Sweden and Denmark had unappealing winter weather. Their rulers weren't known for their art support. The USE Americans already had too much influence in his life. He needed a homegrown solution.

Rubens wouldn't eat anything except bread, cheese, and raw vegetables, with watered wine, a life-long, limited diet, so could not be tempted by the culinary arts. As a substitute, Van Dyck had arranged several of his complete and partially complete *blue paper* works for Rubens to examine. Rubens was a diplomat, in addition to his artistic mastery. He'd been everywhere and dealt with everyone across Europe. If anyone could give good advice, it was Rubens.

Fabrini was a young man, with a young man's perspective. Perhaps he could think of a solution that wouldn't have occurred to older, worldly artists. Van Dyck had a good staff cook. Though his spread couldn't compete with Helene Rubens' feasts, it would be adequate for himself and Fabrini.

When the night of the dinner arrived, all went well, the meal and the portrait exhibition. As expected, Rubens limited himself to bread and cheese, but Anthony provided the best cheese and the finest bread. The vegetables were the cleanest, freshest produce. The great artist praised Van Dyck's portrait skill. Giorgio was delighted to be present with such great talents.

The three settled into fine chairs, with cognac and excellent watered wine in hand. Anthony had ordered the roaring fire that Rubens preferred.

Rubens swirled his wine. "Signore Fabrini, our host has even selected chairs of my own design." He snorted. "*My designs*, to be sure, but stolen by some lesser maker. Anthony, my friend, what has brought on the extravaganza you've produced tonight?"

Van Dyck sighed. "You've seen through my ploy, Peter-Paul. I have a problem. I'm seeking the help of my friends. You two are *one-woman* men. Suddenly, I find myself a *two-woman* man." He explained how his former mistress was refurbishing another house in Antwerp. "I fear that she hasn't given up all claim to me. She still has her looks. I can't pretend that such a claim is totally unwanted."

He then explained that he'd somehow become engaged to Mary Ruthven. "I don't entirely believe her, but if I deny her claim, she might take her *destroyed betrothal* claim to King Ferdinand's magistrates. She has the title *Lady* attached to her name. I may be *Sir* Anthony Van Dyck, but I was knighted by a king who's no friend of Ferdinand or the Dutch. In court, it would be my word against hers. I can obtain no current documentation from England, nor can she. A lawsuit would cost me gold and time, with an uncertain terminal outcome.

"Worse, I know that she's no longer a *Lady*. She's a commoner, who held her title as long she was a queen's lady-in-waiting. Henrietta Maria is dead. Mary Ruthven is no longer *Lady* Mary Ruthven. The thought of marrying her gives me cold feet all the way to my armpits, but she was never my enemy. I'd have to publicly humiliate her, and I don't want that. She's a lovely woman, or I might never have considered marriage.

"That isn't the worst of it. Neither of the women knows about the other. They're in the same city. It's only a matter of time. What will they do to each other, and to me, when they find out? Margaret would see even a bogus engagement as a renewal of my betrayal. Mary would want me to evict a former mistress from my property." Van Dyck, already on his second cognac, was thinking about a third. "I don't know where to turn."

"Have you considered leaving Antwerp for, say, a less threatening location?" Rubens asked.

"I have, but there are no good options. You've helped me establish myself here. I'd have to rip up my roots and move to some doubtful locale, like Denmark. The stress and my social shortcomings would pursue me to death in a few years, which I'm planning to avoid. Remember how Caravaggio's enemies pursued him until they thought he was dead? I like my life here *as is.* There must be a solution besides faking my own death!"

Giorgio cleared his throat several times. "Signore Van Dyck, pardon me if I speak out of turn. Do you see that your troubles would have been avoided if you'd married a good woman years ago. Perhaps not *these* women, but...well. Herr Rubens and I are the better for having a good woman at home who loves us and whom we love. We have children, who've become the lights of our lives."

Anthony blushed. What the young engraver said was too true. He'd considered that artists were above conventional morality. He'd even fathered a child by another model, both of whom had died. Middle-aged, he was looking for stability himself. That didn't solve his current problem. Silence shadowed the trio.

Rubens spoke at last. "Have you noticed that Spain hasn't come marching across France to attack Ferdinand, the Dutch, the USE, or the Swedes—all of whom Spain hates? Why not?"

Anthony thumbed his chin beard. "Hmmm. Spain has gotten itself too involved in the papal succession in Italy. It also has overseas colonies that give it trouble. Why do you bring that up?"

"Spain is distracted. Its attention is on anything but a war it would like to fight. You have to transfer those women's attention to something besides making your life miserable. That was a masterful move, getting Margaret Lemon focused on managing property away from you. When she discovers

Mary Ruthven, her attention will shift to *making war* on you again. You have to act. You have to make your moves before they can make theirs.

"Consider Mary Ruthven. She's desperate, putting on a false front. She's hoping that you don't realize she's not a *Lady* anymore. Her life in England crumbled to pieces. If she can get you to the altar soon, that won't matter. She wants marriage, stability, and safety. You're the only target she has to obtain those now. You need to find her another target. You need to find her a *papal succession* to stop her stalking you."

Giorgio Fabrini looked directly at Anthony. "Signore Van Dyck, Herr Rubens has given you better advice than I could. Don't forget what I said, though. You *will* escape these problems. When you do, look about for the good thing that Herr Rubens and I have in our lives. The hour grows late. Your guests need to return to their wife and families. Herr Rubens will be staying in Antwerp tonight, rather than risk the nighttime roads, but his carriage can drop me at my house." The problem seemed to be settled for now, as much as it could be. Van Dyck shook hands with his guests in the American fashion as they departed. Van Dyck was still too troubled to invite his friend, Peter-Paul, to stay in his large house.

* * *

Dreams are filled with wispy, colorful scenes and symbolism, especially for an artist, to whom multicolored artistry is second nature. Sometimes, though, the sleeping brain grinds away at a problem that has stymied the waking mind. It was better that he'd forgone that third cognac. Antony van Dyck awoke with a formulated plan, similar to his on-the-spot solution to Margaret Lemon's abrupt reappearance.

He breakfasted and dressed slowly. There was no hurry. Margaret preferred the semi-luxury of sleeping late, though she was a ball of energy into the night. The butler prepared his carriage. The cross-town trip wasn't lengthy, but he didn't push for speed.

Margaret was at her morning meal when he arrived in *Kasteel van Rijsel*'s foyer. The newly hired majordomo seated him there with a glass of good wine. The mistress of the house prepared herself. Her dress would be business-like, but her makeup had to be carefully applied. A woman doesn't go into battle half-armed. Any meeting with Anthony van Dyck was a kind of battle.

She wasn't even slightly prepared for what he had to say. She'd barely heard about Mary Ruthven while in England. By his own admission, she'd also heard nothing about betrothal negotiations. She was unaware of Lady Ruthven's Antwerp presence, nor about her claim to be engaged to Anthony. Not one item pleased her.

Van Dyck had taken Rubens advice: He'd moved on Margaret before she could move on him. He drew her into his plot. Since she hadn't originated the scheme, she was carried along with it, unprepared.

* * *

Lady Mary Ruthven was surprised when a *Three Oaks Inn* servant informed her that another English lady had come calling. Few knew she was in Antwerp. Fewer knew her well enough to call on her. The newcomer was well-dressed, if not richly dressed. They retreated to a private room off the inn's main dining room. Once seated, the caller introduced herself.

"I'm Margaret Lemon, Sir Anthony van Dyck's business manager and official hostess. Sir Anthony will be hosting a gathering at his *Stadt van Ghent* manse. He intends that the gathering introduce you to his circle of Antwerp friends. I'll act as hostess and provide genteel music for Sir Anthony and his guests."

Mary assessed the woman across from her. Business manager? Official hostess? Oh, yes. Certainly. But the caller was far too pretty to act *only* those roles for Anthony van Dyck. Margaret similarly assessed Lady Mary Ruthven. At twenty-one, she was at the pinnacle of her beauty. She was at home with courtly manners, dress, and speech. Considering her claim to nobility, Van Dyck might readily have chosen to drop Margaret and to marry into higher status. If Lady Ruthven hadn't tried so abruptly to thrust herself on Anthony, she might have been serious competition. Sir Anthony van Dyck might well have found himself altar-bound. Competition? What was she thinking? She'd been too much in demand from other artists to tie herself to one, especially one as flighty and unfaithful as Anthony van Dyck.

"Lady Ruthven, Sir Anthony instructed me to escort you to him today. He's at Vosterman's engraving studio. We three are to have a meal together. There's excellent dining at a hotel's restaurant nearby. Would you care to accept?"

Mary wasn't about to refuse a chance to connect to Anthony van Dyck. She especially didn't want to have him enjoy a companionable meal with his pretty *business manager.* "That sounds like a lovely idea. You will give me a few minutes to prepare myself? I would thus be close to my fiancé," *Get the message?* "and it would help us renew our acquaintance before the nuptials." *If you didn't get it the first time, try that, Miss Lemon!*

"That would certainly be no problem."

Mary excused herself and hurried to her quarters. She'd meet the reluctant Sir Anthony with the proper dress, the correct hair, and the right makeup. She made the entirely-too-pretty Margaret Lemon wait close to an hour as she and her maid prepared. That was its own reward.

Van Dyck's carriage waited for the pair. Transition to the engraving studio went as smoothly as rough streets would allow. The women wouldn't arrive with muddy skirts. Vosterman himself was waiting to greet them. He was well-dressed, as a professional should be. His hair was somewhat unkempt, and his pointed beard was more developed than Van Dyck's. He was nevertheless a well-proportioned, middle-aged man. He bowed over each woman's hand. Though he'd never met Margaret, he'd engraved a sylvan scene in which she'd been a central figure. Lady Ruthven wore nobility as elegantly as she wore her court dress.

"I apologize, my ladies, but Sir Anthony is no longer present. He was called away to an emergency at Herr Rubens' estate. He won't return to the city until tomorrow. However, he persuaded me to accompany you to the prepared dinner, if that's acceptable." It hadn't required much persuasion for Vosterman to agree to consume a fine, free meal in the presence of two beautiful women.

Margaret readily agreed. Mary was swept along by momentum. She wasn't so flush with funds as to turn down an elegant meal, paid for by the man she planned to marry. The hotel, with its superior dining, wasn't far, but the carriage underlined their class. They were expected. The waiter-in-chief showed them to a choice table. The wine arrived before the fine, pre-ordered meal.

Abruptly, Margaret looked stricken. "Ooh!" She clutched her midriff. "I'm suddenly unwell." She groaned. "Probably bad water. I'm yet new to Antwerp myself." She doubled over, apparently in pain. "I fear I'm struck with *traveler's delight.*" She clutched Mary's forearm. "Please forgive me. I fear I must retreat to my lodgings. Please, do go on. The food here is too good to miss. I must take the carriage, but I'll send it back for you." She rose briskly and walked toward the exit, clutching her stomach.

Mary blinked several times. "Well—I suppose."

"Do stay, Lady Ruthven. It would be inconvenient to depart now," Vosterman said.

"Very well, Herr Vosterman." She glanced about and sighed. Mary wouldn't miss Margaret Lemon excessively. Her current location was superior enough to fit her supposed status.

"Do call me 'Lucas,' Lady Ruthven. I am an old friend and business partner of Anthony's. We will see much of each other."

"Oh. Very well. Tell me more of your acquaintance, *Lucas*, as we enjoy this fine wine."

Oddly, the excellent meal was long arriving. The waiters, however, were constantly attentive. They continually refilled empty wine goblets. By the time the food arrived, she'd allowed Lucas to address her as 'Mary.' The food was as good as promised, and the conversation was enticing. Vosterman regaled her with his adventures, especially those of escaping England. That brought on a sadness, when he described his wife's death.

"My son, Lucas, is my apprentice. He has a brother and sister at home." He sighed.

Touched, she sought to distract him. She described her own plight and her strained exodus from Charles I's court. She even admitted that she was no longer strictly a *Lady.* That's what allowed her to become "Mary" for him. The second bottle of wine was as good as the first. The afternoon waned toward sunset before they remembered the waiting carriage. The wine also dissolved any suspicions about too many coincidences.

* * *

Anthony van Dyck's note was short, obviously written in haste. *Mary, the crisis at Herr Rubens' estate continues to be complicated. It requires my presence for possibly days more. I have arranged for you to pose for some sketches for Herr Vosterman at his residence. He will be creating a spread of engravings of you, as a gift from me. I will see you next at the gathering at my residence. Contact Miss Lemon if you have any difficulties. Affectionately yours, Anthony van Dyck.*

She was already planning the clothes and makeup for her *coming out* party. If she didn't know better, she would have sworn that Sir Anthony was avoiding her. He'd been so solicitous in acknowledging her that such *couldn't* be the case. He'd provided not only a memorable dinner but also the carriage to carry her to Herr Vosterman's residence.

Herr Vosterman met her and kissed her hand, instead of merely bowing over it. "It's so good of you to come. My engraving studio is a noisy madhouse. Anthony thought my home studio would be better for some quiet sketches."

"Herr Vosterman—"

"Please. Not long ago we were 'Lucas' and 'Mary.' May we not be so again?"

"Oh—Very well." She blushed. How much had she said to this man during a long afternoon and too much wine? She barely remembered,

He stared at her. "Would that I could capture that lovely blush with an etching. Metal is so crude to try to duplicate such beautiful features."

She blushed again. "Nonsense! I've seen your engravings. They're the finest art on their own. You don't need Anthony van Dyck and his paints." Why did the sound of *you don't need Anthony van Dyck* echo in her head?

"Come. Let us adjourn to my studio. You will stay for a meal with us afterward, won't you? My children would love to meet you. Anthony has sent me a superb ham and some top quality vegetables, just for the occasion." He half-bowed and gestured toward his studio.

It was small, but well-lighted. She posed on a tall, padded stool as he sketched. Of necessity, he needed to stare for extended periods at both her profiles and her face's full front. She was twenty-one and a *Lady* from a queen's court. She'd never appeared more attractive. He found himself more than once staring instead of sketching. Finally, he shook himself.

"You have a slight blemish on one cheek, but be certain that will never appear on my engraving to mar your perfection." She blushed again. He wished that he could capture that pinkish highlight, but a mere sketch was too crude a medium. "Come. I'll introduce my children before we dine."

He led her through the house to a withdrawing room. He signaled his elderly maid to summon the children.

His son Lucas was twelve, but he obviously thought himself a young man instead of a child. He bowed stiffly and courteously. Hans was about nine and Katrina was a bouncy six or seven. The boy made an awkward bow, but Katrina rushed forward to touch the fabric of Mary's dress.

She looked up into the visitor's face. "Your dress is so pretty, and you're so pretty, too!" Katrina's own dress fit her awkwardly and her hair was slightly disheveled. Mary, who'd dressed a queen and arranged royal hair, itched to lift the girl's appearance to a higher standard. She was such a handsome, precocious child!

They adjourned to the laden table. Vosterman carved the ham himself. All had wine, though Hans' and Katrina's were watered. Her host explained, "Hans and Katrina each actually have five names, but I like the shortened ones, in the American style."

The meal was good, and the company was better than good. She stayed two hours longer than necessary. Once again, too much wine caused her to hug Hans and Katrina before departing. Lucas III placed a sloppy, wine-stained kiss on her hand, as did his father. Lucas Vosterman's sober kiss on her hand seemed to linger.

* * *

Margaret Lemon found reason to dine with Mary at the *Three Oaks Inn*, "settling last-minute details for the gathering." There was little to settle. Mary needed only to know about the dinner seating arrangements. She would sit between Sir Anthony and Lucas Vosterman. The dinner party wouldn't be as heavily attended as Mary had expected.

With time on their hands, they began to talk about men. Mary had had only limited male contact at court. Margaret, the more experienced, had little good to say about Sir Anthony van Dyck. He was an unstable, skirt-chasing artist. Yes, he was well off now, but he had no head for money. Worse, he would probably be unfaithful to Mary about five minutes after the nuptials.

Lucas Vosterman, on the other hand, was a stable family man, who would soon have a substantial income. He had an adorable, pointed beard, but someone needed to help him with his hair and clothing. As a widower, he might soon be looking for a wife. Margaret, a good actress, looked wistful. Mary, out of her depth without realizing it, looked thoughtful.

* * *

Only Peter-Paul Rubens and his wife Helene were present, with Giorgio Fabrini and his pregnant wife. Van Dyck, out of courtesy, had invited Lucas Vosterman, though he had no escort. Margaret played beautifully on the harpsichord and intoned a haunting melody on the flute-like recorder.

At the dinner itself, Anthony seated himself beside Mary, with Lucas on the other side. The group had no more than settled, than a servant rushed to Van Dyck's side and whispered in his ear.

"Really!" Van Dyck shot to his feet. "An emergency has occurred, which I must see to in person. I sincerely apologize. I'll try to be back presently. Margaret will see to your needs." He hurried from the room. The servant followed, trying to keep the silver pieces in his pocket from jingling.

The group was left to converse among themselves. Helene Rubens was interested only in the food, a paltry seven courses. Rubens ate his usual almost nothing. Fabrini spoke some with Rubens, but he saw Vosterman daily. They had little to say that hadn't already been said. He also had to hover around his wife. Giselda didn't yet speak either English or Flemish well. That left Lucas and Mary in quiet conversation as the meal ended. Neither was impressed with Anthony's lack of manners. His behavior lately seemed entirely too much like dodging his responsibilities toward Mary. They left early, despite Margaret's best efforts as a substitute host.

Lucas essayed to hold Mary's hand, in comfort for her worry about her unstable situation.

* * *

A courier arrived to deliver a verbal message to Mary at the *Three Oaks Inn.* "A letter has been left for you at Lucas Vosterman's engraving studio." That was the total extent of the communication. The messenger shifted from foot to foot, body language hinting for a tip. None was forthcoming from the upset woman. She even had to rent her own carriage. Nothing about the situation pointed toward a hopeful outcome.

Lucas Vosterman handed the letter to her in person. "Anthony paid no attention to me when I pointed out his rudeness. Will you read it now?"

She was trembling. "Yes. Yes, I think I'd better. This cannot be good news." He stood close, ready to support her.

My Dear Lady Mary Ruthven: You should consider our doubtful engagement to be suspended until I am able to obtain documentation from England to confirm it. Do not attempt to take this matter to the magistrates. I would see it disseminated widely that your nobility has vanished with the queen's death. I don't believe we should meet in person until further notice. Sincerely yours, Anthony van Dyck.

Her whole plan had come to nothing, like a ship ripping its belly on hidden rocks in darkness! She blushed and paled alternately. She would have struck the floor in a faint if Lucas Vosterman hadn't guided her to a couch, with his supporting arms around her. She burst into tears. Whatever would she do? She wept on his shoulder. His arms hadn't moved, though he'd scooped up the letter and read it.

"The bounder! I'll have satisfaction from that man for his mistreatment of you!"

"No. No," she sniffed. "He's right. I'm no longer a *Lady*. What must you think of me? My father is a doctor, not a noble."

"What does that matter? I've known about your situation almost from the first. I'm a common engraver myself, no more noble than a ditch-digger."

"Common? You? Ditch-digger? You're one of the most talented men I know. But my betrothal—"

"It meant nothing to Anthony van Dyck. To me, its cancellation means that you are a free woman."

"Free? Free to sink into poverty and misery, perhaps."

"No, free that I may request that you become my wife. That foolish painter has discarded a treasure. I would be a fool not to pick it up." He kissed the tears from her cheeks. His beard tickled, but she didn't mind. Other kisses followed, not on the cheek.

* * *

Anthony van Dyck had invited Giorgio Fabrini to dine with him at his home. Fabrini had accepted reluctantly, not wanting to offend his mentor, Lucas Vosterman.

"Giorgio, I've invited you here because I want you to act as my advocate with Lucas. I can engrave well myself, but my love is painting. I want to get back to that, without distraction. My friend, Vosterman, never caught onto what was actually going on. I had a beautiful fiancée on my hands, whom I didn't want to marry. I could see my friend Lucas sinking into sorrowing widowerhood, ruining his work. Here is what I and Margaret did..."

When Van Dyck had finished, Giorgio burst into laughter. "That is the cleverest—" He clapped his hands in happiness. "Yes! Yes, I'll speak to Lucas for you. We have to rescue this friendship. With Rubens' huge talent and yours, and Vosterman's engraving, we'll dominate the entire Antwerp school of art. We can't let misplaced animosity spoil that. I'll begin right away." He bounced up, shook hands, and hurried from the house.

* * *

Margaret Lemon was entirely satisfied. She stood beside Van Dyck's fireplace, a glass of wine in hand. "I never saw a plot work out so well. Vosterman has a beautiful bride. Mary Ruthven is out of your hair. She still thinks of me as a confidante, despite your demotion to dirt beneath her feet. Everything is finally settled."

"Not quite." He rose to stand beside her. "I'm rich now. My patrons pay on time, unlike King Charles. I have all the commissions I can handle, though I'm noted for my fast output. Nevertheless, I envy Rubens and Fabrini. I come home to an empty house every night. I was a fool to abandon you in England. You are beautiful, true, but you have the business sense that I lack and have no time for. I would rather you moved to *Stadt van Ghent* as my wife."

Suspicion blossomed across her face. "What? You know I'm not a virgin, and you weren't my first artist. I'm a commoner, and you're the noted *Sir* Anthony van Dyke. I can still model for Jordaens or Brouwer." She gulped her wine. "Would I keep *Kasteel van Rijssel?* You've been noted to change your mind when the artistic winds blow wrong."

"Yes. It's yours. Finish its reclamation. It will give you a place to retreat if I become too, uh, unspeakable. I'm not a spring chicken, covered with down, anymore. I plan to sink my roots in Antwerp and never leave it. If I must travel to some golden patron, you'll come with me. If you model for Jordaens or Brouwer, that will be *modeling* only. I know you. You know me. Grow together with me here." His arms went around her.

"I don't—I'm not—" She dropped her wine glass, to shatter on the hearth. That certified her answer as she kissed him back.

Available Now

Mrs. Flannery's Flowers

Bethanne Kim

Mrs. Flannery's Flowers
Bethanne Kim

Big things are happening in Grantville since it was sent through time and space to war-torn seventeenth-century Germany, and up-timer nursing student Krystal Reed isn't handling it very well. She never wanted to live in Grantville and being sent back to the seventeenth century just makes it worse. Working with doctors who think bleeding is a legitimate medical practice and that women have no business in medicine is exasperating, to say the least—but their prejudices are no match for the new medical programs in Grantville and Jena. Now if only she can recover from losing her parents, her friends, her home, her college, and her future.

Nils Jorgensen and family are just a few of the thousands of down-timers looking for a new future in Grantville. They arrive with little more than their skills. Through hard work, the Jorgensens start a fashion empire.

For the elderly Irene Flannery, life is more about smaller, personal issues. With no family left up-time, her biggest worry now that she's in the seventeenth century is having a married curate at the Catholic church. (The scandal!) But she has kept a secret since FDR was President and she'll defend her rose bushes to the death because of it.

https://www.baen.com/mrs-flannery-s-flowers.html

The Gourmets Of Grantville

Bethanne Kim

The Gourmets Of Grantville

Bethanne Kim

After traveling through time and space from 2000 in West Virginia to 1631 in Germany, the Grantvillers have to find enough food, medicine, and other supplies to stay alive and healthy while helping their new German neighbors and a constant flow of refugees do the same. Working together, they grow and gather enough food for everyone, but it's not quite what anyone is used to eating. Down-time Germans view potatoes as animal food, unfit for human consumption—until they try their first potato chips. Seeing everyone, including small children, drinking beer instead of water is a big change for the up-timers, just as big a change as seeing people casually drink water and not get sick is for down-timers. But the Grantville Cooking Club proves food is also a bridge, helping up-timers and down-timers work together to create a new cuisine. They also jump-start several new restaurants and businesses.

Meanwhile, regular life continues. How do you keep going when you know that your child, or spouse, will die because life-saving medicine or surgery isn't available in 1631? How do you cope with watching them slowly die from something that was curable, before? Greg Ferrara, Linda Bartolli, and Phillip Bartolli are forced to face these questions when the Ring of Fire happens weeks before Tina was scheduled for lifesaving surgery that, like her life-saving medication, is no longer available.

And what do you do when your wife really wants a bagel with cream cheese but they haven't been invented yet?

https://www.baen.com/gourmets-of-grantville.html

Red Shield

Bethanne Kim

Red Shield

Bethanne Kim

Big battles may be fought with APCs and battleships, but when a small West Virginia town goes back through time and space to land in Thuringia, Germany in 1631, there are bigger battles to fight. Ones the military might struggle with. The kind meant for octogenarians, parents, and teens. Whether their goal is preserving the past, ensuring the future, or making the world a better place, these volunteers aren't going to accept "it can't be done" as the answer.

Some of their goals may sound simple—teaching hand washing for Pete's sake!—but the missions of the Red Cross and Scouts have never been more important, and their tools more in need of evolving, to win the hearts and minds of the new world that surrounds them than in the 1630s.

No matter what the tool or the fight, Grantvillers are ready for battle and the world better "Be Prepared" for *Stayin' Alive* West Virginia style!

https://www.baen.com/red-shield.html

The Marshals

Mike Watson

The Marshals

Mike Watson

The New United States is about to join the United States of Europe, becoming the State of Thuringia and Franconia. The Thirty Years' War is still being waged. Armies cross and re-cross the German states. With war comes lawlessness, and with lawlessness comes the need for law and order.

Who can fill this enforcement niche better than three retired old soldiers, known to down-timers as *Die Drei Alten Soldaten?* Archie Mitchell, Harley Thomas, Max Huffman, retired US Army master sergeants who, with their apprentice, Dieter Issler, use their up-time experience as deputy sheriffs to become the first Marshals of the newly created District Court system of the SoTF.

The Marshals are little known until Thomas Bloem and his sister, Maria D'Angelo, brother and sister journalists, arrive to interview them. They record the formation of the Marshal's Service and the three Marshals, from their first case as Marion County Deputy Sheriffs, until they leave Grantville to provide law and order throughout the State of Thuringia and Franconia.

https://www.baen.com/the-marshalls.html

Time Spike: The Mysterious Mesa

Garrett W. Vance

Time Spike: The Mysterious Mesa

Garrett W. Vance

The time-twisting Assiti Shards are the distressing consequences of a highly advanced and completely insane alien race's idea of art. One of the shards has struck in the southern Illinois region, thrusting peoples from different historical eras into the middle of one of the most dangerous periods ever known: The Cretaceous! Lost in a nightmare world, a conquistador from the year 1541 finds a U.S. Cavalry Scout from 1838 hanging helplessly from a snare. The Spaniard frees him, an act of mercy leading to an uneasy alliance. After battling a "dragon" we know as the Tyrannosaurus Rex, they find themselves in the shadows of the Cyclopean pyramids of Cahokia, the greatest city of the forgotten Mississippian civilization. The Rattlesnake Priests prepare a grisly celebration for their reptilian god, but thanks to the intervention of the Raven Priestess, they escape the city with a pair of Pre-Mound tribesmen who invite the castaways from the future to join them in their beleaguered village. They find the villagers trying to defend themselves from the giant creatures roaming this primeval land. Thankfully, a new hope can be seen across the vast, dry flats of the Drained Sea—a mysterious mesa rising more than a thousand feet into the sky, another bizarre result of the unnatural disaster. Could this be a haven? To find out, the four newfound friends set out on a journey that will prove to be more dangerous than anything they have faced yet!

https://www.baen.com/time-spike-the-mysterious-mesa.html

Coming Soon

Flint's Shards, Inc.

Time Spike: The First Cavalry Of The Cretaceous

Garrett W. Vance

Time Spike: The First Cavalry Of The Cretaceous

Garrett W. Vance

The unlikely foursome of an AWOL US cavalry scout, a repentant conquistador, and two young chiefs of a neolithic pre-mounds tribe have formed a friendship and alliance that breaks the bonds of centuries and cultures. They are now the 'dragon'-slaying four Great Chiefs of the young Mesa Peoples and Allied Tribes, a human civilization growing against steep odds in the Earth's Cretaceous Period (introduced in *Time Spike: The Mysterious Mesa).*

These bold heroes now face a formidable foe, not the enormous dinosaurs that roam this ancient world, but other humans! The rapacious Rattlesnake Cult from the City of the Pyramids has laid siege to Stone Wall Village. Only the newly-minted First Cavalry of the Cretaceous, brave pre-mounds warriors astride a prehistoric equine species native to Pleistocene North America have a chance of saving their kinfolk and restoring peace and prosperity in the lush and deadly *New* New World. Here comes the cavalry!

Published: 3/3/2026

https://www.baen.com/time-spike-first-cavalry-of-the-cretaceous.html

March 2026 Baen Bundle (dissolves March 2):

https://www.baen.com/w202603-march-2026-monthly-baen-bundle.html

Saving The Dodo

Garrett W. Vance

Saving the Dodo

Garrett W. Vance

This book is an extensive rewrite and expansion of "Second Chance Bird."

Every American knows about the poor dodo, the veritable poster child of wildlife extinction. When Caroline Platzer explains the bird's total extinction to her young charge, Princess Kristina, the very upset princess is determined to do something about it—and it may not be too late! The last recorded sighting of the dodo was in 1662 and now it is only the year of our lord 1635. Maybe, just maybe . . .

Enter Pam Miller, Grantville's resident birdwatcher and nature lover. When asked by Princess Kristina to lead a mission to the distant Indian Ocean Isle of Mauritius to prevent the hapless dodo's inevitable extinction, Pam agrees. Wasn't saving the dodo one of her own childhood dreams? Now, thanks to the Ring of Fire, maybe she actually can! She and Princess Kristina hatch a plan, bonded by their mutual love for the natural world.

The whole thing will be terribly risky, a long journey in a sailing ship around the Horn of Africa and out into the still mostly unexplored vastness of the Southern Indian Ocean. Can Pam Miller really save the dodo? Can she save herself and her companions from the multitude of threats they will face along the way? The only thing Pam knows for sure is that this is her chance to change history, and an ungainly flightless bird is counting on her.

Published: 4/7/2026

https://www.baen.com/saving-the-dodo.html

April 2026 Baen Bundle:

https://www.baen.com/w202604-april-2026-monthly-baen-bundle.html

I Want To Be Your Hero

Kerryn Offord

I Want To Be Your Hero

Kerryn Offord

Coming May 5, 2026

https://www.baen.com/i-want-to-be-your-hero.html

May 2026 Baen Bundle:

https://www.baen.com/w202605-may-2026-monthly-baen-bundle.html

* * *

Up-Time Pride And Down-Time Prejudice

Mark Huston

Up-Time Pride And Down-Time Prejudice

Mark Huston

Coming May 5, 2026

https://www.baen.com/up-time-pride-and-down-time-prejudice-2026.html

May 2026 Baen Bundle:

https://www.baen.com/w202605-may-2026-monthly-baen-bundle.html

1637: Pilgrim's Passage

Eric Flint and Griffin Barber

1637: Pilgrim's Passage
Eric Flint and Griffin Barber

The Ring of Fire Series Returns with Conflict and Intrigue in the Middle East!

The more things change, the more they stay the same. . . .

Jahanara Begum is on pilgrimage, a journey and rite every Muslim must essay if able. The up-timers of the USE Mission are escorting the princess in her travels to Jeddah before returning home, their mission accomplished and allies made of the court of Dara Shikoh, having helped to place him on the Peacock Throne.

But the pilgrimage is only the public-facing reason for her departure from Agra.

In reality, the begum sahib is also carrying her love child off to Jeddah in hopes of giving birth in secrecy. Everyone outside the Mission and her most loyal followers must be kept ignorant of the impending birth, a feat which would be hard enough if her brother hadn't saddled her with the presence of her great aunt and frequent adversary, the sometime empress Nur Jahan.

If the presence of her most brilliant adversary in her court wasn't enough, a Mughal princess abroad is an important figure, and the political situation in the Hijaz—a complex of relations between Ottoman Bey, Sharif of the Hijaz, the Bedouin, and Persian interests—is about to boil over.

Can Jahanara Begum and her USE allies safely navigate the power politics of the Pilgrim's Passage?

Coming August 4, 2026

https://www.baen.com/1637-the-pilgrim-s-passage.html

To be included in the August 2026 Baen Bundle

Supporting the 1632verse

We appreciate our readers, and we thank you for continuing to support the 1632 universe. None of the things in this section are likely to be news to most of our readers, but here are some ways you can support us more.

Reviews

This is pretty straight-forward: Books that have more reviews (especially positive ones) are promoted more, so we need our readers to review our books.

So pretty please and thank you, take a minute to review this book. And if you leave a comment in addition to stars, know that we will read it and we appreciate the time you take for those comments!

Give a 1632 Gift

1632 is a free download from Baen. Issue 1 of Eric Flint's 1632 & Beyond is a free download on 1632Magazine.com and Baen. Please share them with anyone you think might get hooked!

You can give (or receive) a gift subscription to 1632 & Beyond. Just choose "gift" when you add it to your cart.

We also have some branded items available to buy on our Zazzle store. There is a coffee mug with the Hangman Regiment logo, an Apple watch band with a becky (currency), and a wine bottle tote with the cover from Issue 2. We hope you find something fun you enjoy! If you have a suggestion for something new, just let us know and there's a good chance we'll add it.

https://www.zazzle.com/store/1632_and_beyond

Buy Another Issue

There are 102 volumes of the Grantville Gazette and a new issue of 1632 & Beyond every other month. That's a lot! Have you read them all? If not, bundles of six (one year of the magazine) are a great way to save some money. They are priced at six for the cost of five.

Buy a 1632 Baen Novel

The Grantville Gazette and now Eric Flint's 1632 & Beyond are the short story venues for the 1632verse and Baen publishes the novels. While we (obviously) benefit more directly from magazine purchases, we still benefit indirectly when you buy novels from Baen. Some of us also benefit directly as authors receiving royalties.

The Baen books fall roughly into two camps right now. First, the mainline novels. These are generally the ones released in hardback and then paperback in addition to ebooks. (Again, roughly speaking.) Then there are the ebook only releases. As of 2026, the majority of these were originally published by Ring of Fire Press, but there are two fully new novels (*Security Solutions* by Bjorn Hasseler and *Red Shield* by Bethanne Kim). Baen has provided new covers and polished all the former RoFP novels a bit more before re-releasing them.

There are dozens of mainline books from Baen. The link below lists them all by publication date. There are also links to a list chronological within the universe and one by storyline.

https://author.1632magazine.com/canon-continuity/1632-books-by-publication-date/

Connect with us on Social Media

We would love to hear from you here at *Eric Flint's 1632 & Beyond!* There are lots of ways to get in touch with us and we look forward to hearing from you.

Main Sites

Email: 1632Magazine@1632Magazine.com

Shop: 1632Magazine.com

Author Site: Author.1632Magazine.com

For anyone interested in writing in the 1632verse, or fans interested in more background on the series and how we keep track of everything.

Facebook

Our Facebook Group is our primary social media, but we do use the FB Page, YouTube, and Flickr accounts.

Facebook Group: The Grantville Gazette / 1632 & Beyond

We also have a Facebook Page at Facebook.com/t1632andBeyond.

YouTube

We have quite a lot on our YouTube Channel because we have videos of most of the panels from at least four separate 1632 Minicons, including FenCon in 2025, FantaSci in 2024, and several with Eric and other now-deceased authors on the panels. In addition, we have playlists with videos of Mannington, the town Grantville was based on. We know we have an international readership, so one of the playlists shows real estate listings for typical Mannington homes, to give y'all a more realistic idea of what they really look like.

YouTube: 1632andBeyond

Flickr

These images are mostly of Mannington, WV, the town Grantville is based on. There are a lot more ranchers, trailers, and other humble, normal homes than this may lead you to expect because, well, it's more fun to share photos of a freshly remodeled painted lady than a double-wide with a pickup and two ATVs in the yard.

https://www.flickr.com/photos/199556693@N05/albums

Reviews and More

You are welcome to join us on **BaensBar.net**. Most of the chatting about 1632 on the Bar is in the 1632 Tech forum. If you want to read and comment on possible future stories, check out 1632 Slush (stories) and 1632 Slush Comments on BaensBar.net.

Last but far from least, if you are interested in writing in the 1632 universe, that's fabulous! Please visit **Author.1632Magazine.com** (QR code) for more information.

Circling back to the very first way to help: Reviews really matter, especially for small publishers and indie authors, so please take a few minutes to post a review online or wherever you find books, and don't forget to tell your friends to check us out!

www.ingramcontent.com/pod-product-compliance
Lightning Source LLC
LaVergne TN
LVHW010654110826
845149LV00014B/3091

* 9 7 8 1 9 6 2 3 9 8 3 6 7 *